"Miss Jennifer Hale?"

Jennifer stiffened as the deep voice rasped over her nerve endings. She didn't have to turn around to picture the owner. She knew *exactly* what he looked like—tall, dark and domineering. Why me? she brooded, turning to find her nose level with the third button of his shirt.

The low rumble continued. "I'm Dave McGraw."

"You can't be," she blurted, looking up into a lean, tanned face.

"Why not?"

Because she had expected someone pale and drawn. Because the eccentric gray-haired woman on the plane—Dave McGraw's Aunt Tillie—had said her nephew had a heart problem and that she was coming to take care of him. She had definitely given Jennifer the impression that her nephew was an invalid, not a man bursting with health— and hormones!

Dear Reader,

Welcome to Silhouette—experience the magic of the wonderful world where two people fall in love. Meet heroines that will make you cheer for their happiness, and heroes (be they the boy next door or a handsome, mysterious stranger) that will win your heart. Silhouette Romance reflects the magic of love—sweeping you away with books that will make you laugh and cry, heartwarming, poignant stories that will move you time and time again.

In the coming months we're publishing romances by many of your all-time favorites, such as Diana Palmer, Brittany Young, Sondra Stanford and Annette Broadrick. Your response to these authors and our other Silhouette Romance authors has served as a touchstone for us, and we're pleased to bring you more books with Silhouette's distinctive medley of charm, wit and—above all—*romance*.

I hope you enjoy this book and the many stories to come. Experience the magic!

Sincerely,

Tara Hughes
Senior Editor
Silhouette Books

RITA RAINVILLE

No Way to Treat a Lady

Silhouette *Romance*

Published by Silhouette Books New York

America's Publisher of Contemporary Romance

To literacy tutors all over the world.
To all of those who give so much
at the Long Beach Laubach Literacy Council.
And especially, to Avis Broxholme,
Frances Varnell and Peter Ramirez,
the three special people who trained me,
thus preparing me for one of the most
heartwarming experiences of my life.

SILHOUETTE BOOKS
300 E. 42nd St., New York, N.Y. 10017

ISBN: 0-373-08663-6

First Silhouette Books printing July 1989

RITA RAINVILLE

has been a favorite with romance readers since the publication of her first book, *Challenge the Devil*, in 1984. More recently, she won the Romance Writers of America Golden Medallion Award for *It Takes a Thief*. She was also a part of the Silhouette Romance Homecoming Celebration, as one of the authors featured in the Month of Continuing Stars.

Rita has always been in love with books, especially romances. In fact, because reading has always been such an important part of her life, she has become a literacy volunteer and now teaches reading to those who have yet to discover the pleasure of a good book.

Southern California is home to this prolific and happily married author, who plans to continue writing romances for a long time to come.

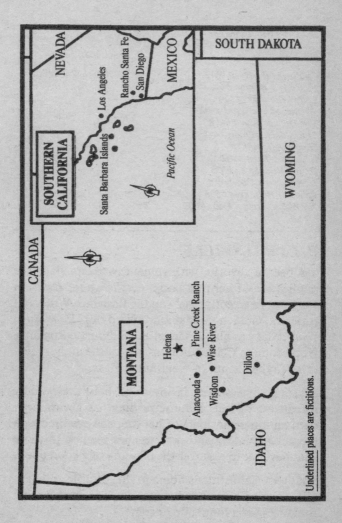

Underlined places are fictitious.

Chapter One

He was trouble. In spades. She knew it at a glance.

"Well, thank God he isn't *my* trouble."

Jennifer Hale muttered the thought aloud when she spotted the big, prowling, black-eyed man enter the baggage area of the Butte airport. He was dark—from his tan face, slightly shaggy black hair and trimmed mustache all the way down to his gleaming cowboy boots—and that made him seem even bigger.

Her lips curved in a complacent little smile as his long-legged stride made mincemeat of the distance between the door and the far end of the room. Some other woman would have the dubious pleasure of dealing with his seething energy and the renegade quality that no doubt fluttered any number of feminine hearts. Any, that is, except hers. The woman he was meeting—and she had no doubts that it would be a woman—was welcome to him.

Because, she, Jennifer Hale, had had more than her share of large men, some of whom even moved with his catlike grace. Her father, Charles, had been one of them. So had her three brothers—Luke, John and Paul. The four of them had towered over her and smothered her in a mantle of masculine protection, ignoring her protests and demands for independence. Eventually, with murmurs of encouragement, they'd turned her over to another man cut from almost the same mold. Richard, her husband.

Ex-husband.

Enough of that, she told herself. She was free. *Free*. For a whole year now, she had been on her own. And she could spare a compassionate thought or two for the poor soul who was being picked up by the black-eyed devil impatiently curling the brim of the cowboy hat he held in his large hands. Curious, she scanned the room, automatically eliminating the males, the elderly, the infirm and women above or below a certain age. That didn't leave many, she realized with interest. The blonde over there—no, his gaze just went past her. Maybe the one in tight jeans, with brown hair. Nope. He didn't even blink.

More curious now, she turned her back to him so she could look at the rest of the room from his perspective. It wasn't all that big and there weren't that many people milling around, so it didn't take long. *That* was the one, she decided, settling on a sultry brunette with lush curves and a pouting mouth. Good. She looked as if she could handle him. Or at least hold her own.

Relieved, Jennifer slanted a quick look over her shoulder at the cowboy. She wanted to see the expression on his face when he spotted the curvy menace. Standing in her little niche, Jennifer didn't question the surge of curiosity she felt about the big man. Watching strangers was an innocent game she often played. God only knew she'd had enough practice at it when she had been married to Richard. At parties, more often than not, he'd left her to fend for herself while he'd conducted business.

There! If she had been an instant later, she would have missed it. Jerking her thoughts away from her ex-husband, she watched the cowboy's eyes stop moving, go into reverse and zero in on the brunette. One thick brow shot up in speculation, then lips moved beneath a midnight mustache, pursing in a silent whistle.

Jennifer blinked at his purely masculine gleam of appreciation. Wrong again, she decided, as his gaze moved on after a distinct pause. Darn. What a waste. They were both a bit larger than life; they would have been perfect for each other. Apparently the brunette thought so, too, because her smoldering gaze was following every move the cowboy was making. Dismissing the woman with another blink of her lashes, Jennifer turned back to the last possible candidate, regarding the petite blonde with an empathetic frown.

No, not her, she thought with a rush of sympathy. Anyone but her. She looked too...vulnerable. As if life had already whacked her a good one and she was just now finding her feet. The slim young woman didn't look any more capable of handling that human volcano than...than she, herself, would be.

That was one thing that Jennifer had no illusions about. She was not a fighter. At least not until she had exhausted every other option and her back was to the wall. Her divorce was a case in point. It had taken her two years to admit that Richard was more than reserved, that he was, in fact, a pompous, judgmental bore. It had taken another year to convince herself that giving her usual hundred and fifty percent was not going to cure a marriage that never should have happened, and a final year to convince *him*. She sighed, thinking of his weekly letters. She had a sneaking suspicion that he still thought she'd be coming back and was trying to make her first step in his direction an easy one. Although, why he wanted her back was anybody's guess. She certainly hadn't fit the mold of—

"Miss Hale?"

Jennifer stiffened as the deep voice rasped over her nerve endings. She didn't have to turn around to picture the owner of the voice. She knew exactly what he looked like—tall, dark and domineering, with go-to-hell eyes.

"Miss *Jennifer* Hale?"

Why me? she brooded morosely, turning with reluctance and finding her nose even with the third button of his dark blue shirt. Life just wasn't fair. Not only was it not fair, she decided, it had one hell of a sense of humor. She had traveled from California to Montana to do a good deed and this was her reward?

The low rumble continued. "I'm Dave McGraw."

"You can't be," she blurted, looking up into the lean, tanned face.

He cocked an interested brow. "Why not?"

Because she had expected someone pale and drawn. Because the fascinating and eccentric little gray-haired

woman she had sat next to on the plane—Dave Mc-
Graw's Aunt Tillie—had said that her nephew had a
heart problem and that she was coming to take care of
him. Aunt Tillie had accepted that Jennifer's destination was the same as hers without a hint of surprise: Dave McGraw's guest ranch. In fact, if Jennifer
hadn't known better, she would have thought that the
delightful, if somewhat scatty, old woman had known
that fact before she had even mentioned it. At any
rate, she had definitely given Jennifer the impression
that her nephew was an invalid. Not a man bursting
with health—and hormones.

Dave dropped his hat on his head and stuffed his
hands in the back pockets of his jeans while he
watched Jennifer Hale's expressive face. She wasn't
what he had expected. Not by a long shot. Teetering
back on the heels of his boots, he mentally reviewed
what he had been told about her. She was a teacher,
retired he had thought. And she was staying at his
ranch while she helped establish a literacy council in
the area. Teachers were obviously retiring earlier these
days.

She was a far cry from the altruistic senior citizen he
had pictured. And she didn't look like any teacher he
had ever had. Some of them had pulled their hair
back, but none had achieved such an elegant, swirly
knot. And none of them had possessed such a mass of
tawny hair, blue eyes big enough to fall into and lips
that begged to be kissed. Nor had any of them walked
around in a body that was pure provocation, even
when it was covered with pleated slacks and a prim silk
blouse.

Though his eyes didn't move from her face, he managed to catalog everything else that was important. The top of her head came up to his chin, which put her at about five foot five, and he couldn't think of how even one of those sixty-five inches could be improved. As he continued to stare down at her, two thoughts occurred to him. There *was* one thing he would change. He'd get rid of the wary look in her eyes. She was watching him the same way a rabbit eyed a snake and he didn't like it. Not a bit.

The other thing was, he hoped she didn't plan to buy into many poker games. Because, so far, she hadn't had a thought that wasn't written all over her face. For some reason, she had expected someone entirely different. That was obvious. And she didn't like what she was seeing—that came across loud and clear.

"Have you seen a little gray-haired woman around here?" he asked abruptly. "Stands about this high?" His hand came to a halt at a point level with Jennifer's eyebrows.

"Curly hair? Wears, uh, interesting clothes?"

His nod was a blend of affection and resignation.

"Aunt Tillie?" Jennifer ventured.

"You met her, I take it."

Jennifer nodded. "I sat next to her on the plane. Interesting lady."

Interesting? He narrowed his eyes, examining Jennifer's expression. She meant it. After a second's thought, he agreed. Aunt Tillie was that, all right. She was also different. Lovable. Weird.

"Is her husband waiting for her at the ranch?" Jennifer asked idly.

Dave felt every single muscle in his body stiffen. "Did she say he was?" he asked cautiously, hoping that Jennifer's answer would be a definite and resounding negative.

Frowning, trying to remember exactly what the older woman had told her and wondering why Dave McGraw seemed to be holding his breath as he waited, Jennifer remained silent. "She told me she hoped to see him while she was at the ranch," she finally said.

Dave relaxed. Hoping was one thing, actually *seeing* the man was a horse of another color. He knew for a fact that Uncle Walter had died twelve years ago. He had flown to California for the funeral and had held Aunt Tillie in his arms, sharing his strength, offering consolation to the tiny woman who was so lavish with her love.

A few months later, he recalled, he had received the first of many letters from his cousin, Kara Brady. Uncle Walter, although he may have passed on to another plane, didn't allow such an insignificant happening to slow him down. He was still in constant communication with Aunt Tillie. In fact, he was quite a busy man. He advised Aunt Tillie about the fluctuating stock market and passed on a continual stream of suggestions and warnings to the rest of the family.

Dave himself had been the recipient of one of Walter's dire predictions. Grudgingly, more to satisfy an anxious Aunt Tillie than because he believed, he had cut his hay three days early. Later, on the day he had planned to do it, he had stood in his office and watched hailstones the size of golf balls tear into the earth.

Dave shook his head. Uncle Walter wasn't at the ranch. Or, he amended cautiously after a moment's thought, if he was, he was no more visible than Aunt Tillie was at this very moment.

He scanned the rapidly emptying room impatiently, verifying what he already knew. There was no petite woman draped in yards of colorful material anywhere in sight. "Where did she go? In there?" he asked hopefully, pointing in the direction of the ladies' rest room.

Jennifer shook her head slowly. "I think she went to look for a store."

"She's shopping?" Dave stared down at her in disbelief. "She hasn't been in town ten minutes and she's shopping?"

"Maybe she wanted to buy you a gift," Jennifer murmured soothingly. She was proud of her calm voice. Jennifer was an accomplished soother. It was one of the talents she had honed to perfection during her four years with Richard.

"I don't *need* a gift," he informed her bluntly. "What I need is her, right here." He pointed with his index finger to a spot on the floor in front of him. Rubbing at a sudden knot of tension on the back of his neck, Dave reminded himself of Tillie's propensity for finding trouble. If it was anywhere around, she'd be in the middle of it.

"She'll be right back," Jennifer said in the same tranquil voice, biting back a smile. Dave McGraw was obviously a bachelor, a man without the least understanding of how much pleasure a woman took in giving to the people she loved. And there was no doubt that the delightful little woman loved her nephew. It rang in her every word.

"Although," Jennifer added in sudden doubt, remembering exactly how little the old woman was, "she may need some help carrying it."

"Carrying what?"

"Your gift."

Dave exhaled sharply. He smelled trouble and this woman, with her soft voice and big eyes, wasn't making things any better. "Just what did she go looking for?" he asked evenly.

"A saddle."

He stared down at her. "A *saddle*? You don't just march into a gift store and buy someone a saddle. Besides, I've got a whole tack room full of them."

"Not this kind."

"What kind?" he demanded.

Jennifer mentally asked Tillie's forgiveness for spoiling her surprise and said simply, "A silver one."

The knot slid from Dave's nape to the pit of his stomach, growing larger and colder with every inch it moved. "Tell me *exactly* what Aunt Tillie said before she left," he ordered.

Jennifer blinked as his expression shifted and became relentlessly grim. "She said she had to find a silver saddle."

Dave swore softly, succinctly. "That was all she said?" he finally asked.

She nodded. "What's the matter?" she gasped as he took her elbow and nudged her toward the front door.

Instead of answering, he called to one of the men on duty. "Amos, will you watch this stuff until I get back?'' He pointed to a heap of luggage that Jennifer had been guarding.

''Sure thing, Dave,'' the balding man said amiably.

Before she knew what was happening, Jennifer found herself being bustled out the door into the blazing July sun. It was easier to go along quietly than to argue the point, she assured herself. Especially since he was twice her weight and, in sheer bulk, probably twice her size. Besides, he was her host. She could trust him. Then she slanted a quick look up at his grim face and had second thoughts. Digging her heels into the pavement, she demanded breathlessly, ''Where on earth are we going?''

''To find Aunt Tillie.''

''But she's just shop—''

''She isn't,'' he said flatly, steering her toward a new but dusty pickup truck. Opening the door, he waited while she got in, snapped, ''Buckle up!'' and slammed the door. Seconds later he was settled behind the wheel and putting the powerful machine into reverse.

''What if she comes back while we're gone?'' Jennifer asked, warily eyeing the cowboy who took up more than his share of space.

''She won't.''

''You seem awfully sure,'' Jennifer protested, picturing Tillie lugging a saddle back to the airport and finding no one waiting.

''I am.'' Dave pulled up for a red light and looked down at the woman sitting next to him. She didn't like being hustled away from the airport and he couldn't really blame her. She deserved an explanation, and he'd love to give her one, but he had never figured out just how to explain the fey, enchanting woman that was his aunt.

Sighing sharply, he asked, "While you two were on the plane, what did you talk about?"

Jennifer shrugged. "The usual. The weather, our mutual destination, things like that."

"Did she seem surprised to hear that you were coming to the ranch?"

"No." She said the word slowly, wondering what he was getting at. "I thought it was a little odd at the time."

"Odd. Peculiar. Strange. Those are all words that have been applied to Aunt Tillie at one time or another. Do you believe in psychics?" he demanded abruptly.

Jennifer narrowed her eyes, puzzled by the non sequitur. "I think so. Of course, I've never known anyone who—"

"You do now."

Sitting up straighter, she turned her head and stared at him. "Are you telling me that your Aunt Tillie is—"

"Psychic."

"Are you sure?" she ventured, finally breaking the silence in the truck. "She seems so, so..."

"Normal?" His voice was wry.

"Well." She drew out the word with a reluctant smile. "I was going to say charming."

"She's that all right. But I grew up around her, lived with her for a couple of years, and I'm here to tell you, honey, that she's a genuine, gold-plated psychic."

Fascinated, Jennifer stared at him. "You really mean it, don't you?"

He nodded.

"How does it work? Does she see things? Hear voices? What?"

Dave shrugged. "Damned if I know. And I don't really want to, anyway. What I *do* know is that twelve years ago, when her husband died, the burden suddenly seemed too much for her. She stopped predicting things and started having daily conversations with Uncle Walter. He became sort of a scapegoat, responsible for any bad news. I can't explain it, but I'll tell you this, the whole family snaps to attention when she starts a conversation by saying 'Walter said.' "

Walter said that David would be having trouble with his heart, and I'm going to the ranch to take care of him. Jennifer heard Tillie's chatty voice as clearly as she'd heard it on the plane earlier that afternoon.

"Is she ever wrong?"

Frowning thoughtfully, Dave shook his head. "Hardly ever."

"What else does she do?" Jennifer asked faintly.

Dave's smile was not comforting. "She recently volunteered to be a subject for a parapsychology research team at a nearby college. She wrote and told me all about it. She knocked them for a loop when they discovered that she could consistently identify cards that were facedown on a table."

"You mean playing cards?"

He nodded again. "Every one in the deck. Time after time, so there was no chance of it being a fluke."

"That's all very interesting," Jennifer said carefully, "but I still don't understand why we're hotfooting it away from the airport."

"Because she developed an interest in cards and certain gambling is legal in Montana."

"Was that an explanation?" Jennifer asked in confusion, wincing as Dave barreled around a gray sedan driven by a conscientious observer of the speed limit. "Because, if it was—"

"And the Silver Saddle is a saloon in a less than desirable part of town."

"Uh-oh."

"Where an even less than desirable element gathers to play some very serious poker."

"Oh dear," she murmured inadequately.

"I couldn't have said it better myself." He pulled up in front of a weathered building whose sign sported a spotty, peeling saddle. "Come on, let's get in there."

"I've never been in a place like this," she said, giving it a dubious look. "Especially in the middle of the day."

He slammed his door and came around to her side. "It'll be good experience for you," he said bracingly. "As a teacher, you need to broaden your horizons." He held out his hand and waited.

Jennifer released her seat belt and reluctantly placed her hand in his. "I teach children," she informed him energetically, ignoring the devilish smile that made his mustache twitch, "and I can't think of one thing that they'll gain from this."

As she turned on the seat toward him, Dave stepped in closer. Settling his hands on her waist, he tugged gently. When her feet touched the ground, he slowly let her go and moved back an inch or two. Before she could move, he draped an arm around her shoulders and aimed her toward the swinging doors.

Taking a deep, ragged breath, Jennifer moved woodenly beside him, fighting the reaction that had jolted her body. A year, she thought, dazed. It was almost a year to the day that she had left Richard. And not once in that time had she wanted more from a man than friendship. She hadn't even *thought* about it. Now, at merely the touch of this cowboy's hands, the heat from his body, she was melting, struggling for breath because his arm held her against his hard frame.

Before she had time to come to terms with the feelings rampaging through her body, they were in a dimly lit room. Several men with faces roughened by sun and hard weather lounged at the wooden bar, each propping a foot on the brass rail. Even as she looked around in interest, she felt Dave's deep breath, heard his muttered oath. Responding to the hand tightening on her shoulder, she looked up at him, then slowly turned her head to follow the direction of his gaze.

Aunt Tillie, her short silvery curls gleaming from the light of a hanging lamp, sat at a round table with a mound of money in front of her, talking animatedly to four tough-looking men. Dave tensed and Jennifer bit back a gurgle of laughter.

The four men sat with identical, bemused expressions, occasionally glancing at each other in pained communication. They looked, Jennifer thought, like Saint Bernards confronted by a dazzling humming-bird. Tillie was in the same garment of peacock blue and green that she had traveled in. It was held together by a mauve rope belt. Orange high-top tennis shoes with purple laces peeked out from beneath the table. Wisps of frothy material trailed in the air as she gesticulated.

"Now, Jerry," she said in a soft, breathless voice, "you just told me that four of the same card beats almost anything. You can't keep changing the rules every time we play a new game."

"Almost," the man reminded her wearily. "*Almost* everything." He looked at one of the other men. "You tell her, Mike."

"Ma'am, your four bullets—" he pointed to the aces turned up in front of her "—aren't any good if he has a straight flush."

Tillie stared at him uncomprehendingly.

"Oh, hell, Mike," a third man grumbled, "she don't know a flush from a full house. *Show* her."

Mike obligingly reached across the table and arranged Jerry's handful of hearts in ascending numerical order. Tillie watched with unblinking concentration. "See, ma'am? He's got a seven, eight, nine, ten, jack. That's the straight part. And they're all hearts. That's the flush part."

"Yes," she murmured, a puzzled frown drawing her silvery brows together, "but—"

"There ain't no 'buts' about it," the third man interrupted. "Jerry won, fair and square."

Tillie tilted her head and regarded him with bright blue eyes. Then she looked over her shoulder at the couple standing frozen in the doorway. "Ah, David dear," she said vaguely. "You found Jennifer. I've been expecting you. I'll be through in just a minute."

"Aunt Tillie," Dave began in a determined voice.

"In a minute, dear. When I'm through with these nice men."

"Nice, my...foot," he muttered, removing his arm from around Jennifer's shoulders and positioning himself in front of her.

Jennifer watched his massive shoulders flex as he took a deep, bracing breath. He was, she realized, prepared to launch himself at the table and extricate his aunt at the first sign of trouble. Moving slightly, she angled to one side where she could watch the five players.

Tillie turned her guileless blue gaze back to Mike. "Thank you," she said gently. "I understand the straight part and the flush part, but—"

"Good," the third man said. "Jerry wins. Let's get on with the game."

"But what I don't understand," Tillie said, ignoring the interruption, "is how he can have a ten of hearts *there* when I have one *here*." She placed her last card on the table, faceup. "And I don't know why he has a ten of clubs on his knee."

In the grim silence that followed, she placidly scooped the money from the center of the table and added it to her stack. Pulling a woven purse that matched her mauve belt out of the folds of material, she filled it with her winnings and stood up. Beaming down at the four sullen men, she said agreeably, "What an interesting game this is. There's always something new to learn."

After tucking the purse back within the depths of cloth, she trotted over to her speechless nephew, turned up her cheek for a kiss and waited. Dave managed to keep one eye on the four luckless gamblers while he touched his lips to her smooth skin.

Muttering beneath his breath, he wrapped one hand around her elbow, the other one around Jennifer's, and hustled the two women outside. "Aunt Tillie!" he exploded when he had stuffed them into the cab of the truck and moved out into the traffic, "those guys were crooks."

A smug smile crossed her lips. "I know. Isn't it exciting? I can't wait to tell Walter."

Scowling down at her, Dave repeated his words, spacing them for emphasis. "They were crooks."

"Not very good ones," she said comfortingly. In the silence that followed, a small frown knitted her peaked brows. "I don't understand the game as well as I thought I did," she admitted finally. "I'm going to have to read my book again."

Jennifer leaned back against the door, prepared to enjoy herself now that Tillie wasn't in any danger. Dave muttered and inhaled noisily.

"You learned to play poker from a book?" he asked evenly.

Tillie nodded. "Of course, Walter explained some of the finer points."

"Years ago you told me that he never gambled."

"He didn't."

"So how could he explain something that he doesn't—didn't—understand?"

"Things change," she said vaguely.

"You mean he gambles now?" he asked in disbelief.

"He *may*," she allowed cautiously. "I don't know for sure. There's a lot of things he doesn't tell me. But I *think* he's hooked into some sort of Universal Knowledge. It's all very confusing. But, if you like, I can ask him the next time I see him,'' she offered brightly.

"When, uh, exactly, do you expect that to be?" Dave asked carefully.

"Today."

"Where?"

"At the ranch, of course."

Dave reached out and took one of her hands in his. "Aunt Tillie," he said gently, "don't set yourself up for a big disappointment. Uncle Walter isn't at the ranch."

Tillie's bright eyes examined her nephew's face, then shifted to take in Jennifer's concerned expression. She patted the younger woman's knee and gave them both a comforting smile. "You just never know," she told them in a placid voice. "Walter shows up in some very unexpected places!"

Chapter Two

Later, Jennifer glanced around her comfortable living room with satisfaction. It would do quite nicely, she decided. Somehow it managed to blend early rustic with homey functional and retain the best of both. And even better than that, she reflected, it didn't have Dave McGraw prowling around within its four walls.

The weathered log cabin was square, larger than she had hoped for. The back half was the bedroom and bath; two-thirds of the front was a cozy living room, with the remaining third a small kitchen. She was either unbelievably lucky, or someone had considered her needs and moved in some suitable furniture. The square tables at either end of the sofa had doors that concealed several shelves, perfect for the brochures and training material she had brought with her. There was even a small desk against the wall, near an electric outlet, which already held her typewriter.

"Hi. How's it going? Getting settled?"

At the sound of the deep voice, Jennifer looked up from where she sat cross-legged on the floor, surrounded by stacks of literature. For a moment, before she'd heard his voice, one part of her brain had registered the fact that the room had darkened abruptly and had wondered if a cloud had obliterated the sun, but now she realized that it was merely Dave, filling the outside door of the cabin. Merely? She questioned her choice of words, eyeing the length and breadth of him. No, hardly that.

He took a long swallow from a bottle of beer and held one out to her. "Want some?"

She nodded, in answer to all his questions. Earlier, he had driven her to the door of the cabin and hauled in her luggage, brushing aside her offer of help. The boxes of material she'd sent ahead had been neatly stacked by the fireplace. She had spent the time since then getting comfortable in what would be her home for the next five or six weeks.

"Come in. Have a seat." She held out one hand for the beer and gestured to the sofa with the other.

When he stepped in, she blinked at the almost feline grace of his large body. She was going to have to do something about that, Jennifer lectured herself. She couldn't go around ogling the poor man every time he moved. She accepted the cold bottle and watched him swing one of the plaid upholstered chairs closer to her before he dropped into it.

Jennifer shifted uneasily on the large braided rug placed between the fireplace and the brown sofa. The matching armchairs filled in the other two sides. The room was reasonably spacious. Or at least it had been until Dave sat down, she thought. Suddenly it seemed to shrink. He definitely took up more than his share of room, she decided, staring at his long, muscular legs encased in jeans, stretched out full length and crossed at the ankles, at the dark boots almost touching her bare knee. Lost in thought, she jumped at his sudden question.

"Is this going to be enough room?"

She looked around again and nodded. "It'll be fine."

"The kitchen's awfully small." He frowned at the compact refrigerator.

"I'm not going to be whipping up large family dinners," she told him dryly. "As long as it holds the fixings for breakfast and lunch, and some soft drinks, it'll do. If your cook is as good as you say she is, I plan to have most of my evening meals up at the lodge."

"You're not going to make a stranger of yourself, are you?" His voice told her what he thought about that idea.

"What do you mean?"

"I mean," he drawled, "you're not going to hole up in your cabin all the time, are you? You haven't even been up to the lodge yet."

She looked at him in mild exasperation. "For heaven's sake, Dave, I've only been here a couple of hours. I'm trying to get all my stuff in order."

"You can do that later. Besides, it shouldn't take you that long to hang up the clothes you brought."

"I finished that in about twenty minutes. It's all this paperwork that's taking the time." She waved her hand at the mound of literacy material. "I have to get it organized."

He shifted in the chair and glanced around. "Right now?"

"Yes."

Well, actually, she admitted to herself, it really didn't have to be done just then, but she *wanted* to do it. Four years of living with Richard in the regimented, sterile atmosphere he'd demanded of his surroundings had left her with a need, almost a compulsive one, to do things in her own time and to leave her own mark on her immediate environment. When she opened the door and stepped into the cabin, she wanted to feel warmth, a sense of belonging. Even after a year she still luxuriated in the knowledge that she wouldn't have someone following her around, giving the place a white-glove inspection. And if the rooms were a little cluttered, so be it. At least they were welcoming, alive.

"Tell you what," Dave suggested, "you tell me where you want things and I'll put them away for you. Then, when we're done, I'll give you the fifty-cent tour of the place." He surged to his feet, ready to sweep her away in a flow of energy.

Torn between the sheer, stubborn need to do things *her* way, in her own time, and the sudden knowledge that she was tired of being cooped up, she gave a reluctant nod. "Okay."

That was all he needed, she realized, watching him move into action. It wasn't that he had walked in planning to take over; it was simply the way he operated. With Dave McGraw, the thought was father to the deed.

He reached down for her hand and tugged her effortlessly to her feet. Pointing to the nearest pile of booklets, he asked, "Where do these go?"

Pulling her hand out of his, she stepped back and pointed. "On the table, over here."

"Okay, I'll bring them over and you pile them in the way you want."

The transfer was quickly made. Only once in the next few minutes, when Jennifer looked up just as he hefted an armload of workbooks, did they slow down. "Should you be doing this?" she asked him when he set them on the table.

He stopped where he was—which was altogether too close for her peace of mind—and stared at her. His eyes weren't really black, she realized with a blink. They were dark brown, highlighted by prisms of gold.

"Doing what?" he asked blankly.

Jennifer shrugged uncomfortably, remembering Tillie's concern about his heart and how he had carried her luggage, lifting it as easily as he would the evening paper. "Carrying these books," she mumbled.

"These?" he asked in astonishment, pointing to the stack he had just set down. She nodded, and he looked from her to the books and back again, wondering out loud what kind of men she normally associated with. When she didn't enlighten him, he grinned reassuringly. "Honey, compared to a bale of hay, these are like toting a couple of feather pillows. Now, what about the rest of that stuff?"

"On the other table," she said, unconvinced. He lifted bales of hay? By himself? She wondered fleetingly what Tillie would have to say about *that*. Ah, well, if he wanted to be a big, tough cowboy, who was she to talk him out of it? Obviously no one. Besides, when she'd left Richard, she'd given up trying to manage men. They were on their own. All of them. They were responsible for themselves. Of course, she thought with a sideways glance as he picked up the last stack, from now on she could simply make sure that there was nothing to "tote" when he was around. Satisfied with that decision and assuring herself that she really wasn't "managing," she arranged the remaining material on the shelves and closed the wooden doors.

"Okay." She stood up and brushed at the bottom of her shorts. "I'm ready for the tour."

"Whoa," he murmured, putting his hand on her arm as she moved past him, bringing her to a halt. "Maybe you'll want to put on something a little, uh, longer, before you go out."

Jennifer's eyes narrowed at his drawled suggestion. The last thing in the world she needed was another man who voiced his disapproval over the clothes she chose to wear. "You don't like my shorts?" she asked with lethal sweetness.

"Honey," he assured her earnestly, "I *love* your shorts. In fact, if they were hiked up a couple of inches more, I'd be even crazier about them. But the fact of the matter is, by the time I show you around and you eat and visit for a while, there's going to be a nip in the air."

She raised her brows and looked out at the bright sunlight, taking first things first. "I had lunch," she told him.

"Dinner," he said succinctly, nudging her toward the bedroom.

Jennifer looked at her watch, then up at him in disbelief. "It's six-thirty! It can't be."

"You're in Montana," he reminded her with a small shrug. "It's summer. It gets dark late." He took another long up-and-down look at her bare arms and legs. "And at dusk the mosquitoes come out."

"I'll change," she said hastily, moving into the bedroom and closing the door behind her.

The fifty-cent tour was pretty comprehensive, she decided later as they followed a bubbling stream that meandered through the property. The ranch was big, covering hundreds of acres, a large, peaceful meadow and part of a rugged mountain covered with pine trees. Dave obligingly stopped at intervals so that she could admire the horses in the corral and watch some grazing llamas. The camellike animals watched them with large, liquid eyes, but casually moved away whenever the two of them came too close.

"Do llamas make good pets?" she asked, observing their stately progress with fascination. "And why so many?"

"They aren't pets," he told her, grinning as she stared back at the curious animals. "We breed them." He eyed her expressive face and waited. He wasn't disappointed.

"You don't *eat* them!" She glared at him as if she expected him to whip out a knife, advance on the nearest one and start hacking.

"Here in Montana we don't do things like you do in California," he told her blandly. "We can't just run down to the corner to a fast-food place, you know. Don't you eat beef?''

"That's different," she argued. "I've never found cows all that attractive. Just look at that darling face," she ordered, pointing to a llama that was edging closer, its tall, pointed ears perking inquisitively in their direction. "And listen!" She tilted her head, enchanted. "They're humming!"

He nodded carelessly. "Uh-huh. They always do that when they're happy. But you should hear the racket they make when they get upset."

"Like when someone's trying to make hamburger out of them?"

He couldn't help it. He grinned again and watched her blue eyes flash fire at him. "Well," he began, "really what we do is—"

"Hey, boss!"

They turned and watched a small, whipcord-thin man head down the slope from the lodge. He had a deep tan and wrinkles carved in the outer corners of his eyes that came from years of working out in the elements.

"You about ready to eat?" he called when he got closer. "Irma says she's going to toss it out if you don't get your, uh—" he looked at Jennifer and noisily cleared his throat "—self up the hill," he finished lamely.

"Jen," Dave said, mercifully cutting in on the old man's red-faced embarrassment, "this is Mac, one of the hands. Mac, Jennifer Hale."

Jen? Jennifer held out her hand and waited while Mac rubbed his on the thigh of his jeans. "Nice to meet you, Mac."

"How do, Miss Jenny." He retrieved his hand and lifted his straw hat about an inch off his head, revealing a bald head with a ragged fringe of sandy hair stretching from ear to ear across the back of his head. "Your name's as pretty as you are," he said, eyeing her appreciatively. "You two going to eat?" he asked again.

Jenny? "Yes," she assured him. "I'm ready to eat anything as long as it isn't a llama."

Mac squinted his faded blue eyes at her. "No problem about that, Miss Jenny. Dave here would peel off our skin with a dull knife if we so much as looked hungry around them. They're bred to be pack animals, nothing else. Anyone tell you different, they're just stringing you a line."

"Oh, really?" She looked up, her gaze colliding with Dave's.

His grin was a teasing flash of white. "Now, honey, you're the one who was worried about eating them, not me. Do I look like I'd sink my teeth into something as young and tender as that?" He pointed at one of the smaller llamas, which was moving with coltish grace.

Honey? What did these people have against using a person's regular name, she wondered, deciding she wasn't about to get into a discussion of Dave McGraw's appetites.

"Boss," Mac said, falling in step beside them and voicing what seemed to be a long-standing complaint, "I don't know what in tarnation this place is coming to."

Dave sighed and looked at him. "What's the matter now?"

"We got this real funny little lady—she just got here today—moseying around peeking in places where she hadn't ought to be. Gave one of the boys a real start when he opened the door to the tack room and almost ran her down."

"That's probably my—"

"Dressed in the damnedest getup I've ever seen. Looks like she ran full tilt into a clothesline full of curtains and ended up wearing everything that fell on her."

"Yeah, that's my—"

"You've had some weird ones here in the past few years, but this one takes the cake."

"What's she doing besides looking around?"

"'Bout an hour ago she was perched on that old tree stump down by the creek with her legs folded under her like a pretzel, staring out at the hills—humming."

Dave glanced sideways at the older man. "Humming." The one word was a statement, not a question.

Mac nodded, a frown on his dark face.

"I don't see any harm in that," Jennifer said, rushing protectively to Tillie's defense. "I hum a lot. Half the time, I'm not even aware that I'm doing it."

Mac squinted at her again. "No harm at all," he agreed. "Usually. I've been known to do it myself. But when I do, there's some ups and downs to it. It has a *tune*. Sort of," he amended conscientiously. "I ain't all that musical. But this little lady's humming just sort of drones on, never going anywhere."

"Oh." Somehow Jennifer wasn't surprised. She could easily picture Aunt Tillie meditating in some isolated place, humming a mantra, in perfect accord with the natural beauty surrounding her.

"How did you happen to see her down there?" Dave asked. "I thought you were working in the barn."

Mac tugged his hat down lower over his eyes. "I just thought somebody ought to keep an eye on her," he said gruffly. "God only knows what kind of a mess she could get herself into, dressed in curtains and all. I followed her around until she settled herself on the tree stump."

"Where were you?" Jennifer asked curiously.

Mac's cheeks reddened. "I stayed behind a big boulder and peeked out at her every now and then." He cleared his throat and looked at Dave. "I best be getting back to the barn. Gotta put another poultice on the chestnut's leg." Tugging at the brim of his hat, he mumbled, "Be seeing you, Miss Jenny."

He took a few steps, then turned around again. "By the way, boss, none of the boys have seen Paladin yet."

Dave nodded in resignation. "He'll turn up before the day's over."

Shaking his head, Mac said, "Some fools just never know when they got it good. You'd think he'd be prancing around, knowing he was in hog heaven, wouldn't you?"

"Who's Paladin?" Jennifer gave a half skip, trying to keep up with Dave's longer stride as they moved toward the lodge.

"A llama."

"Oh." She thought about that for a moment. "Why hog heaven?"

Dave grinned down at her. "He's a male I just bought. We brought him in to...service the females."

"Ah." Jennifer nodded. "A stud."

"If his reputation is to be believed—a superstud. Right now he's getting settled in, getting the feel of the place. Keeping his distance from everyone."

"Why is Mac worried?"

"He likes to keep the assets in sight. A holdover from the old ranching days when rustling was a constant worry."

"Rustling? Llamas?" Jennifer's eyes widened. "Does that sort of thing still go on?"

"Some. We don't worry about it much here because we're pretty far away from things and a truck would have a hard time getting out without being heard. Still, llamas are worth a lot of money, so the possibility's always there. But Mac's the last of a dying breed. He cut his teeth on cattle ranches and remembers when you could lose a whole herd overnight. He's a good man to have around, but he doesn't have much tolerance for modern things."

"I noticed. He didn't have the foggiest idea what Aunt Tillie was doing, did he?"

"I doubt it. Meditating's a bit out of his range of interest. He never watches television and only listens to country music on the radio. Says the news is depressing, and if anything important happens in the world, he'll find out about it soon enough."

"When you think about it, it's not a bad idea," Jennifer said, walking through the door that Dave held open for her.

From the outside, seeing it nestled in a loose circle of pines, the lodge looked like a sprawling log cabin. Inside was a different story. There was nothing rough about it, Jennifer decided after a quick glance. The room they were in was large, cheerful and versatile. Along one wall were a number of polished plank tables and chairs used by the guests and staff at mealtime. Beyond them, behind swinging doors, was a bar with a mirrored wall reflecting tiers of gleaming bottles. To the right of the tables were some well-stocked bookcases with several comfortable chairs nearby for browsers.

The focal point of the room was the large stone fireplace. Scattered around it, encouraging conversation, were groups of couches and easy chairs. The walls were paneled and the colors bright and informal. Comfort was the key message that came across. If the cheerful level of conversation was any indication, Jennifer decided, the message had been received loud and clear.

Tillie, dressed in an even more startling combination of ecru crocheted lace and hot pink sash, sat in one of the chairs, carrying on an animated conversation with a bemused young cowboy. Jennifer smiled at the young man's expression as Dave led her over to one of the tables. When she came to a stop, he pulled out a chair and waited for her to be seated.

She hesitated. "Shouldn't we get your aunt?"

"We are." He turned to the young man. "Nick, why don't you and the lady join us?"

"Sure thing, Dave." He jumped up, brushed back his shaggy blond hair and gallantly offered his arm to Tillie, leading her to the table.

Tillie waited impatiently while Dave performed the introductions. "Nick has been telling me all about Warrior," she told him.

"Paladin, Aunt Tillie," Nick corrected.

Dave's brows rose. "*Aunt* Tillie?" he asked.

Nick grinned. "She adopted me."

"Me, too," Jennifer said complacently.

Dave looked at her. "So we're all one big, happy family?"

"Guess so," she said blithely, ignoring the hint of challenge emanating from him. She didn't need any complications with her sexy host in the coming weeks. It was a lot safer to be his "relative."

"It seems that Warrior should be a happy llama," Tillie murmured, picking up the menu.

"Paladin." The other three spoke at the same time.

"At some time during his life," she murmured, "every man fantasizes about having a harem."

Three heads turned toward Tillie and three sets of eyes regarded her with varying degrees of fascination.

Dave spoke first. "How do *you* know?"

"I'm glad to hear it," Nick said with a wicked smile at Jennifer. "I thought I was a maniac of some sort."

"Who said so?" Jennifer demanded of Tillie.

"Walter." She looked up from her examination of the menu. "He told me that many years ago."

"Maybe he was speaking just for himself," Jennifer suggested, aware of the two identical masculine grins turned on her.

"No, I don't think so." Tillie looked up and met her eyes. "Walter was a student of psychology. He said it was a recurring male fantasy—finding oneself in possession of a harem," she ended sedately, unfolding her napkin and putting it in her lap.

"If that's true, then I guess Mac was right. He said that Paladin should be in hog heaven," Jennifer explained to Nick. As the two men exchanged amused glances, she said dryly, "I take it that you agree." Without waiting for an answer, she turned to Dave and waggled the menu. "What do you recommend?"

"That we all tell Irma to bring us the daily special."

"What is it?" Jennifer asked, noting that neither of the men had even bothered looking at the plasticized sheet.

Dave shrugged. "Who knows? It doesn't really matter, unless you have any particular dislikes or allergies. It's always good."

It was more than that, it was delicious, but Jennifer had a hard time concentrating on the tender prime rib because Dave decided to begin an inquisition just as it arrived.

"What's the first thing you'll do to get this literacy business off the ground?"

"I guess I'll call a couple of women in the area who want to be trained as tutors," Jennifer said, poking her fork into a fluffy baked potato.

Dave tilted his head inquiringly. "Who are they? I probably know them. Maybe I can help you get in touch with them."

"I have their names back at the cabin," she said vaguely. "I'll take care of it. Thanks anyway." He was definitely going to be a problem, she thought with a sigh. He wasn't a man who sat on the sidelines and let other people go about their business. But he was going to have to learn. This was *her* baby and she wanted the satisfaction of setting it up herself.

He stared at her thoughtfully. "What comes after the telephone calls?"

"Visit some of the nearby towns and take a look around, I guess."

"No problem about that," he assured her. "I'll be glad to drive you."

"No."

She saw him blink and knew her voice had been sharp. Sharper than he deserved, she told herself. He wasn't the one who had stifled her for four years, the one who'd demanded that things be done his way and only his way. He wasn't the one who had insisted that he always knew what was right for her, so he shouldn't get a lot of grief for offering to help. He had no idea how determined she was to be independent, to rely on no one beside herself. And, since it was none of his business, he would never know. He'd just have to live with her decisions.

"No," she said again, this time adding a softening, "thanks. I don't really know how I want to approach it. Maybe just wander around, talk to people and get the feel of things for a couple of days. Before I do that, though, I'm going to have to rent a car."

"No, you don't," Dave said. "We have cars just sitting around here rusting." He glared when Nick looked over at him in surprise. "You've got your choice of a pickup or a Buick. All you have to do is keep it gassed up and it's yours."

"Are you sure?" Jennifer asked uncertainly. So much for independence, she thought wryly, but it would save her a lot of money and that wasn't to be sneezed at. "I won't be putting anyone out?"

Dave shook his head. "Not a soul. Just let me know which one you want."

"I've never driven a truck."

"Then it's the Buick, although there's hardly any difference in driving them. The pickup is an automatic shift, too. If you ever have to haul anything, I can show you how to use it."

"Thank you," she said slowly, realizing that keeping him out of her business wasn't going to be easy. He seemed to be operating under the theory that she was on his territory and he just naturally had a part in whatever she did. And she had a nasty feeling that changing Dave McGraw's mind once it was made up rated right up there with turning the tide.

Whoa, old son, Dave told himself, examining the wary look that was back in Jennifer's blue eyes. By the looks of things, this was one skittish lady. *Why* was just one of the interesting things he intended to learn about her. Of course, he decided wryly, if she knew the plans he had in mind for her she'd be more than skittish!

But, right now, all he wanted to do was help her. And by the way she was digging in her heels, it wasn't going to be easy. Damn it, he was just being neighborly. All he'd offered to do was make a few telephone calls and drive her around a bit so she'd have some free time on her hands, he thought in disgust. To spend with him, of course. But *she* didn't know that so there must be some other reason she wanted him to back off.

Apparently she didn't have the least understanding of rural life or of people who lived in sparsely populated areas. Of course, he thought, what can you expect of a native Californian? People out there on the coast grew up zipping around on freeways and talking about things like upward mobility and networking, but they had missed the basics. They didn't know diddly squat about calling in the neighbors and asking for help.

Chapter Three

Were you talking to me?" Jennifer asked, looking up from the thriller she was reading.

Aunt Tillie drew a line through some writing on the piece of paper she held and looked around the room. Finally her eyes settled on Jennifer. "What, dear? Were you talking to me?"

Jennifer blinked at the older woman, a bit confused. She was getting used to feeling that way around Tillie, she realized affectionately. Tillie was intensely curious, had a childlike way of looking at her immediate environment and captivated everyone within sight, but she wasn't always connected to the real world.

"Well, in a way, I was. I guess. I thought you asked me something."

The two women were sitting in the main room of the lodge. The other guests were out hiking, riding or cruising around the countryside, taking in the sights, and the room was empty except for the two of them. Jennifer had been busy for the past three days and had decided that she deserved a holiday—one that didn't include things like riding, hiking and driving. She didn't want to do anything more ambitious than curl up on a comfortable couch and read the latest mystery. Tillie had drifted in later, frequently adding something to the sheet of paper she held and muttering to herself.

"I *was* talking," Tillie admitted after a moment's thought, turning her chair so she faced Jennifer. "But not to you. It comes from living alone."

"What does?" Jennifer asked, putting down her book, perfectly willing to follow what promised to be one of Tillie's typical rambling, open-ended conversations.

"Talking to yourself. Myself. You see, Walter was concerned about the list."

"What list?"

"This one." She held it up and absently fanned herself with it.

"What's on it?" For a fleeting moment Jennifer was bitten by her conscience—she wasn't in the habit of asking such direct questions. She relished her own privacy too much to be intrusive where others were concerned, but she had learned something in the past few days. Tillie not only needed such pumping, she actually seemed to encourage it. She had the habit of dropping a tantalizing statement and then waiting for someone to pick up the verbal ball. The conversation then developed into a diluted version of twenty questions. Jennifer hadn't yet decided if the questions were necessary to keep Tillie on target or if the older woman merely used them as a laborsaving device. Whatever the reason, they seemed to work. And if Tillie didn't want to discuss something, she simply got an abstracted look on her face and drifted out of the room.

"Men are on the list. Or rather their names are." She waved a hand in a circle, encompassing the ranch. "All of the ones who work here. And Irma, the cook, of course. It's so I won't forget anyone, you see." She frowned and stared straight at the wall. "But there's one who isn't on it. I haven't met him yet and I don't know his name. A skinny little bald-headed man. He works here. I think. But if he does, I can't imagine what his job is. Every time I look around he's standing behind a big rock or a tree. Just standing there, not doing a thing."

"Mac?" Jennifer looked away from Tillie's baffled expression and grinned. She could just see him tiptoeing after Tillie, freezing behind trees in an effort not to be seen. Poor Mac.

"Of course! That's it!" Tillie said with relief. "Every time I tried to think of his name, I picked up the image of General MacArthur and I couldn't imagine what *he* had to do with it."

"With what?" Jennifer drew in a deep breath. She wasn't improving with practice. In less than a minute she had lost whatever thread they were following.

Tillie blinked at her in surprise. "The list. Isn't that what we were talking about?"

"Why is Walter worried?" Maybe she'd have better luck working on it from another direction.

"Because it's so important that everyone knows, of course."

"About the list?" she asked cautiously.

Tillie tilted her head, her blue eyes considering. "No," she finally said.

Jennifer stared at the little woman, torn between fascination and frustration. She remembered having the same feeling as a child when she had learned to crochet and had been given a brand-new skein of yarn. She had known that the yarn would pull out smoothly once she tugged on the right thread. All she had to do was find it.

"It's not important that everyone knows about the list," she murmured slowly, feeling her way. But they were supposed to know something. What had Tillie said was on the list? Names. Names of people who worked on the ranch.

"I've got it!" she said triumphantly. "You've made the list of names so you'll be sure that you tell everyone something." She looked expectantly across the small distance separating them.

Tillie nodded placidly. "Isn't that what I said?"

"Maybe." Jennifer sighed. "I'm not really sure. What exactly are you telling them?"

"About David's heart. Walter thought that if everyone knew, and each one did just a little to relieve David's work load, things might not be so bad."

"Aunt Tillie, couldn't Walter be wrong this time?" Jennifer asked gently. "Dave is the picture of health. He doesn't look like he's *ever* been sick, and he certainly doesn't act like he's ill."

Tillie shook her head, setting her silvery curls bouncing. "Walter was very definite on the matter."

"Exactly what did he say?"

"That David was going to be in big trouble with his heart. It was very clear, and he told me more than once."

Jennifer leaned forward, holding Tillie's pensive gaze. "Then don't you think you should tell Dave?"

"Oh my, yes." Tillie nodded energetically. "I most certainly will. When the time is right."

And that, Jennifer thought, was that. Aunt Tillie picked up her list and wandered out of the room, muttering something about looking behind some trees to find that strange little man.

"What do you mean all that's left to eat is cereal and skim milk?"

The next morning Jennifer decided to sample Irma's blueberry waffles for breakfast and walked through the door just in time to hear Dave's disbelieving rumble. Tillie had begun her machinations, she thought, and was tempted to walk right back out, but he spotted her before she could move.

"Come sit with me," he directed from his chair, somehow managing a pleasant look for her while scowling up at the ample woman in orthopedic shoes standing over him with an obstinate look on her face. "Maybe you can make heads or tails of what this crazy female is talking about."

Irma cast an apologetic glance at Jennifer but held her ground. "I'm telling you that the guests ate me out of house and home. All that's left is cereal and—"

"I hate skim milk. I wouldn't even feed it to the pigs."

"You don't have any pigs."

"Well, if I did, I wouldn't."

"It's good for you. Isn't it, Jenny?"

"Uh..." Jennifer looked from one stubborn face to the other and wished she'd settled for her own brand of cereal and nonfat milk. At least she could have eaten it without getting indigestion.

"I don't care if it'll grow hair under my fingernails," Dave said, spacing each word for emphasis. "I won't eat cereal."

Irma winced as his voice grew softer with each word he uttered. "That's all I have," she mumbled, tugging a strand of graying brown hair behind her ear and averting her eyes from his steady gaze.

"You hauled in a truckload of food just three days ago," he reminded her. "How could it all be gone?"

"I must have miscalculated. Besides," she said heroically, "the books I have on nutrition tell me that I've been feeding you all wrong. Everything you eat is loaded with cholesterol. So I decided—"

"That you're going to feed me dry grass and watery milk? Wrong." Without another word, Dave got up and headed for the kitchen.

Irma turned a harassed face to Jennifer. "I told Tillie it wouldn't work. That man likes his food, and lots of it."

"Well, you tried," she said consolingly just as Dave started back toward them.

He handed Irma a half-gallon pitcher filled to the brim. "You overlooked the waffle mix," he said, narrowing his eyes and daring her to give him an argument. "I'll have three. With blueberry syrup." He turned to Jennifer. "How about you?"

She looked at Irma, brows lifted in mute resignation. "The same," she said. "One."

Dave went over to the hot plate and got Jennifer a cup of coffee. "I don't get it," he said, putting it down in front of her. "Irma's been here eight years. What do you suppose got her on this nutrition kick? She's never worried before."

Jennifer shrugged, wondering if she looked as guilty as she felt. "Got me. I'm the new kid on the block, remember?"

"A very busy one, from the looks of it." He frowned at her. "I thought this trip was a combination of business *and* pleasure, but I've hardly seen you these past few days. What have you been up to?"

She added cream and cautiously tasted the steaming coffee. "Contacting people on the phone, mostly, then driving around to talk with them. They're scattered in all directions."

"How did you get names in the first place?"

"Actually, some of your local people started the ball rolling. Three women—Madge Buford, Judi Dimmit and Francie Dullas—contacted the state literacy office and said they were interested in being tutors."

Dave's brows rose. "That's all it took?"

Jennifer nodded. "As with any volunteer organization, the state office wasn't about to let some live ones get away. They contacted me and here I am."

Irma stomped up and dropped a plate in front of each of them. Irritation marked every step she took as she clumped back to the kitchen.

"Wait a minute," Dave said, eyeing Jennifer thoughtfully. "That's a pretty big jump from three women in Montana to you in California. Aren't there any people working on it in this area?"

"Oh, sure," Jennifer said, buttering her waffle. "You've already got councils set up in Browning, Bozeman and Libby."

"Then why send for you? They aren't all that close, but they're a hell of a lot nearer than you were."

Good question, Jennifer thought. Too bad I don't have a nice, pat answer. One that doesn't tell him I'm running away from an overly solicitous ex-husband. "Well," she said carefully, "after a few national conferences, people get to know each other. They knew me, knew that I was planning a trip in this area and so they asked me." Relaxing, confident that she'd bypassed the land mines, enthusiasm warmed her voice. "I have all the qualifications—I'm a supervising tutor trainer—so it worked out just fine."

After swallowing a bite of his waffle, Dave asked, "How long have you been involved in this program?"

"For the past four years. When I taught high school, it wasn't uncommon to have some kids each year who read at third and fourth grade levels. Most of them became dropouts. I realized then that something had to be done for them and all the other sixty-three million people in this country who are functionally illiterate."

Dave reached for the syrup and both of them concentrated on the steaming waffles for a few minutes.

"When did you stop teaching?"

"Four years ago," Jennifer said absently. "I'm currently taking some classes to renew my credential."

"Didn't you like working at the high school level?"

Picking up the two cups, she went over to the hot plate and refilled them. While her back was to him, she said, "I loved it."

He waited until she sat back down. "So why did you quit?"

"I was married," she said flatly. To a throwback who didn't want a working wife. To a man whose conservative firm approved of women doing volunteer work, as long as it left them sufficient time to be a proper company wife.

He looked down at her bare ring finger. "Was?"

"Was." End of discussion.

"Good."

Jennifer stared at him. *"Good?"*

"Uh-huh." He nodded for emphasis. "It would have caused a few problems if you'd shown up here tied to someone else."

Else? "I'm not sure what that's supposed to mean," she began carefully, "but—"

"Just what it sounded like," he assured her.

"I'm not attached to anyone now out of choice, and I don't intend to be in the future." Narrow-eyed, she took in his tolerant expression. "Dave, it's too early in the day to start this kind of thing."

"Would lunch be better? Or dinner?"

"Actually," she admitted, "there *is* no right time. Look," she said earnestly, leaning forward, "I've had enough of ties. Once, I walked blindly into a situation that was bad for me, and it took me four years to get out of it."

"You did the right thing."

"You don't know anything about it," she snapped. "Anyway, that's not the point."

His brows rose. "What is?"

"That I'm not going to get myself in such a fix again." It was better to get it out in the open right now, she reasoned, taking another long look at him. He resembled a sleepy, black-maned lion. A *dangerous*, sleepy, black-maned lion. Three days of trying to avoid him hadn't solved a thing. If he was going to start making possessive noises, she'd better stop him right here.

"Honey, you can't let—"

"My name," she said firmly, "is Jennifer."

"Jen, you can't let one bad apple spoil your whole life. You're too young."

"You're right, I am. That just gives me more years to do what I want to do, when and how I want to do it, without any interference."

Dave leaned back in his chair and stared at her. "He really did a royal number on you, didn't he?" When she didn't answer, his voice sharpened. "Did he hurt you?"

Jennifer blinked. "Physically, you mean?"

He nodded, grim-faced.

"Oh, no. Richard wasn't the physical type." She stopped in annoyance when Dave's eyes gleamed with sudden amusement. "I mean," she said stiffly, "that he wasn't the abusive type. We simply... weren't suited." Ignoring Dave's look of blatant curiosity, she edged the topic of conversation back to where it had begun.

"You should see the three women I'm going to be working with," she told him enthusiastically. "Talk about energy! They're raring to get started."

Dave stared at her thoughtfully, then seemed to relax. "What do you do first?" he asked idly, finishing off the last waffle.

"We want to see how many people we can get together for the training session, so each of them is going to check out the local civic and church groups to see if they need a speaker for their meetings within this next week or so. We've already set several dates. Then I'll go and give a pitch for the program, tell the people some of the literacy statistics, show them the type of material we work with and see if any of them want to volunteer.

"Madge said that maybe she could wangle some community service spots on the local radio and TV stations and Judi's going to contact the newspapers."

"Will that help?" Dave watched the sparkle in Jennifer's eyes as she spoke about their plans. She could talk a tough line when she had to—when she was trying to keep him in his place—but she had more caring and softness in her than she knew what to do with. And he couldn't wait to help her figure it out.

"Will publicity help?" she repeated. "Are you serious? The more we get, the better."

Wondering if he was going to get another flat rejection, he reached in the breast pocket of his shirt and pulled out a piece of paper. "Got a pencil?"

Jennifer dug in her purse and found a ballpoint pen. "Will this do?"

He reached for it and rapidly scribbled several names. After a moment's thought he added a couple more, then handed her the paper. "The top three are editors of the papers, the others are radio station managers. I've done business with them all. If you want to use my name, you can. You can also tell them I'd consider it a personal favor if they'd help you out."

She looked like a wildcat sniffing a baited trap, he thought in exasperation. Giving a careless shrug, he said, "If you can't use the names, then toss them. It doesn't matter one way or another to me." Somehow, he managed to conceal his surge of satisfaction when her fingers closed around the paper.

She put it in her purse and said, "Thanks. This will be a big help. I'll pass on the list to Judi and Madge."

"What else are you scrounging around for?"

"A meeting place. While those three are calling around, they're also asking if anyone has a room we can use for the classes."

"How hard is it going to be to find one?"

"I don't know," she admitted. "We don't need anything fancy. Just a room and some tables and chairs. It'd help to be able to hang some charts on the walls, but we can survive without them. If nothing better comes through, and we don't have too many people, I'll use my cabin."

"Any problems with putting on the classes?"

Jennifer smiled and shook her head. "That's the simple part. I love showing people how easy it is to be a tutor."

"Hey, boss." Nick stuck his head in the door. "Jock is madder than hell and practically tearing the fence down. What do you want us to do?"

Dave set his cup on the table and stood up. Jennifer followed him to the door.

"Who's Jock, and why is he mad?"

Dave kept moving, tossing the words over his shoulder. "He's our other male llama and he doesn't like to see Paladin out there roaming around the females."

"I don't blame him." She followed Dave through the door and down the stairs. "It doesn't sound fair."

"He's had his day in the sun, and he will again." Dave put his hand on the heavy gate.

"I'll get that, boss." Nick ducked under Dave's outstretched arm and swung it open.

Dropping his arm, Dave directed a puzzled glance at the younger man before he turned back to Jennifer. "We don't want to get a lot of inbreeding with the herd, so Jock has to be kept away from most of the females. When certain ones are ready, they'll be put in with him. In the meantime, Paladin has the run of the place."

They reached the high wooden fence surrounding Jock's paddock. The llama stretched his neck through the rails and nipped at a tall, mottled brown male who had the good sense to keep out of reach.

"Paladin?" Jennifer asked, pointing to the llama who was calmly ignoring his penned rival.

Dave nodded. "Nick, try to keep Jock down at the far end of the corral until the other ones move away."

Grimacing, Nick said, "I was afraid you'd say that. He's so mad he's probably ready to spit on the first thing that comes close to him."

"Better you than me," Dave said heartlessly. "Think of it this way. If he does, you get to go in and take a shower."

Jennifer watched Nick cautiously open the gate, pick up an old blanket and gradually work the enraged llama down to the far end. Dave walked toward the other animals and they ambled on, coming to a stop a couple of hundred yards away.

He strode back to where Jennifer was waiting just as a heartfelt curse came from Nick's direction. Grinning down at her, he said, "Looks like Nick got hit."

She looked at the young cowboy stomping away, apparently as furious as the llama he was herding. "Is it really that bad?"

"Worse. You can't believe how rank it is. The only thing you can do is get out of your clothes as fast as you can and take a shower."

"Poor Nick."

Dave snorted. "He'll survive." He draped an arm over her shoulders and turned her back toward the lodge. "What do you want to do this evening?"

Startled, she looked up. "I don't know. What are my options?"

"Stay in your cabin alone," he said promptly, as if he'd given the matter a lot of thought, "or invite me over. Of course, you can always mingle with the others in the lodge. I don't recommend that one. Or we can eat at the lodge, then go to my place. That's what I vote for."

"You don't live in the lodge?" she asked in surprise.

"Nope. I need time to myself. A place to spread out and relax." He pointed to a building with a steep, sloping roof that was set beneath some tall pines several hundred yards away. "That's it."

Torn between prudence and curiosity, Jennifer allowed her gaze to linger on the house. It looked like Dave, she decided. Sturdy, stable, unmovable, with an unexpected element of style. Before she had to admit that curiosity was winning, John, a college student working on the ranch for the summer, met them at the heavy wooden gate.

He beat them to it by a good three feet and swung it back before Dave's hand reached the crossbar. "I got it, boss."

Dave looked at him quizzically. "You the official gate opener now?"

"I just happened to meet you here," he said defensively.

"With bad news, I suppose."

"Some. It could be worse. The cutter bar broke on the swather again."

"Hell."

"I take it that's bad?" Jennifer asked. For all the sense the words had made to her, John's statement could have been something out of a foreign language phrase book.

"It means that the haying stops until the bar is fixed," Dave explained. "I'd better get out there again. We may get some rain later."

"Again?" Jennifer looked at her watch. It wasn't even nine yet.

"You didn't think I was just starting my day, did you? We've been out there since the crack of dawn. I just came in for some breakfast."

"Boss, Dean says you don't have to hurry. He's down in the toolshed working on the blade. He'll call you when it's fixed."

"I'll go down and see if he needs any help."

John put his hand out and caught Dave's arm. "Dean's doing just fine. You know how he likes to work alone."

"Since when?"

"I don't know," John said, looking harassed. "He just told me to leave him alone until he got it fixed. Oh, by the way, Mac is looking for you. He wants you to swing by the barn when you have a chance."

"Has the chestnut taken a turn for the worse?"

John shrugged. "Got me. He just said to make it as soon as you can."

Dave looked at Jennifer with raised brows. "Want to come with me?"

"Okay." Actually, she wouldn't have missed it for the world. She couldn't wait to hear the next episode of Mac's adventures.

"Mac? Where are you?" They stepped into the dim interior of the barn and looked around. Jennifer sniffed, picking out the sweet smell of hay, leather and an unidentified medicinal odor.

"Boss! Am I glad to see you!" Mac charged out of one of the stalls and strode toward them, concern written all over his face.

Dave looked around. "Is one of the horses hurt?"

Mac blinked. "Horses?" he asked, thrown off stride. "Naw, they're fine. It's that little lady in the curtains. I tell you, boss, she's up to something. Something fierce."

Drawing in an exasperated breath, Dave moved closer to the old man, and Jennifer sat down on a small wooden stool, preparing to enjoy herself.

"Mac, it's all right, she's my—"

"I've been mulling it over and I think it's all a cover," Mac said, giving a decisive nod. "She walks around looking like she's got a couple of bobbins loose and no one would suspect her, would they?"

"Of what?" The two words came out between clenched teeth.

"Rustling." Mac waited expectantly. He wasn't disappointed.

"Rustling?"

The old man leaned back against a wooden post and nodded. "Yep."

"Rustling *what*, for God's sake?"

"The llamas."

"I don't believe this." Dave found another stool and sat down beside Jennifer. "Mac, have you been working out in the sun again?"

"Boss, she hypnotizes them. I tell you, I've watched her. She goes out every day and sits on that old tree stump and hums, and pretty soon they're all gathered around her. And you know what *they* do?"

Speechless, Dave shook his head.

"They hum *back* at her. And you know what Maybelle—ornery old Maybelle—did this morning?"

"At this point, I'd believe just about anything," Dave muttered.

"Well, you know how standoffish she is? She went over and stood next to her and nudged her on the shoulder, friendlylike! You know what I think?"

Dave shook his head again, beyond words.

"I think she's getting them all softened up, then when the time comes, she's just going to lead them away like the Pied Piper!"

Chapter Four

Dave stared out of the large bay window across the wide expanse of grass to Jennifer's cabin, listening to the distant mutter of thunder. She was late. Not that he was counting, of course. Who was he kidding? he wondered, shaking his head with disgust. The last time he'd looked at the old-fashioned wall clock was exactly two minutes ago.

As he watched, her door opened and she stepped out, locking it behind her. His approving gaze slid over her. She had put away her prim silk blouses—for good, he hoped. Her pleated slacks had joined them. And she had quit tying her hair back. Tonight she was wearing sandals, a knit shirt and white jeans that would test the sanctity of a monk.

She turned and looked slowly around, reminding him of a curious but fastidious cat, intent on absorbing the beauty about her. The sky with its billowing dark clouds held her gaze for long moments, then, seeming to recollect herself, she moved in his direction. As she walked, she gave the impression of savoring every step as she touched the spiky needles of the pine trees, rested a hand on the rough wood of the rail fence and smiled as the llamas turned their heads to watch her pass. He could tell when the breeze quickened; she stopped and ran her hands through her hair, lifting it at the back, exposing her nape. She arched her back in a supple movement and his body tightened, reacting to the unconscious sensuality of the gesture.

How could one woman—a fairly small one, at that—turn his life upside down in one short week? Seven days ago, if someone had told him that he'd be pacing the floor until a woman stepped on his porch and knocked at his door, he would have laughed. Now, he wasn't even smiling. Of course, seven days ago he hadn't known what he was looking for, and he'd thought that Ms. Jennifer Hale was a contemporary of Aunt Tillie's.

Seven days ago, he'd driven into Butte wondering about the curious sense of restlessness that had plagued him so often lately. He should be a contented man, he'd told himself. After eight years, Pine Creek Ranch was almost the way he'd originally pictured it, a prosperous enterprise, busy during each of the four seasons. The llamas were healthy and brought in a substantial amount of cash. He wasn't bored, he enjoyed the challenges that presented themselves on a day-to-day basis. He was just . . . restless.

Several hours later, he'd driven home with Aunt Tillie and the woman whose appearance had clarified the reason for his vague dissatisfaction. He had been waiting. For a woman. No, he'd amended, for *the* woman. Now Jennifer had arrived and his waiting was over. It was as simple as that. Unfortunately, she didn't look at it the same way. And what was worse, nothing seemed to be simple when it came to dealing with her.

Even a blind man could see that she hadn't come out here looking for a man or a new home. Every strand of that gorgeous tawny hair would probably stand on end at the thought. No, what she seemed to want was lots of independence and space of her own.

The only encouraging note was in her reaction to him. She was definitely wary, and that meant that she was reacting to him—and resisting every step of the way. She wouldn't be nearly so concerned if she disliked him. As it was, she walked softly and seemed to be looking for a big stick. Still, she was coming to see him. The wildcat was sniffing at the bait, he told himself grimly, but whether or not she'd reach out and snatch it was anybody's guess.

"Dave?" Jennifer rapped on the screen door and wondered again what she was doing walking up his steps and waiting for him to come and smile at her. She needed that sexy, knock-'em-dead kind of smile just about as much as she needed another Richard in her life. No, what she really needed, she decided grimly, was to have her head examined. Trouble was all she could expect, visiting a man who bristled with potential for complicating her life.

For example, once he had mentioned his house, she'd known he wouldn't let it drop. She had spent the day gearing herself up for the moment he would invite her over. She had planned to explain that she was busy and indicate that she would continue to be busy. But when the big moment came, what had she done? Forgotten every argument she'd mustered up and said yes. That definitely wasn't the way to discourage a man who was beginning to make proprietary noises.

But, of course, there was the chance that she was mistaken, she thought, striving to be fair. That she was imagining things. It was just possible that he was lonely, too. That he had no intentions of complicating the situation, that all he was looking for was friendship. And if that were the case, she'd be a fool to sit in her cabin night after night by herself.

Cheered by that little bit of rationalization, she raised her hand to knock again at the same moment Dave pushed open the screen and smiled down at her.

"I thought I told you to just walk in."

"You did," she said calmly, ignoring the thump in the region of her heart. "I prefer to knock."

"And to have people knock on your door?" he guessed, touching her shoulder and leading her straight to the kitchen.

"Exactly."

Opening the refrigerator, he asked, "What'll it be, iced tea, soda pop or something stronger?"

"Tea, please. That's my summer drink." She perched on a stool and propped her elbows on the bar, watching him stretch out a long arm for a glass. His pale blue shirt pulled taut at the shoulders and clung to the lean length of his back. His jeans had the soft look that came with repeated washings and the fit left little to the imagination. There was no wasted movement when he dropped the ice cubes in the glass and poured the tea. Dave was as comfortable in the kitchen as he was working outdoors, she thought idly. Not all men were. Richard hadn't been.

He handed her the glass, snagged a bottle of beer for himself and said, "I have several new tapes for the VCR. Are you in the mood for a movie?"

She followed him out of the room, asking cautiously, "You're not a devotee of chainsaw massacres and violent sex, are you?"

Stopping in the middle of the doorway, he turned and looked at her. "Have I given you the impression that I would be?"

Jennifer stared straight ahead at a broad chest. When she lifted her gaze a notch, the chest was topped by broader shoulders, a strong neck, a tanned, expressionless face and dark, waiting eyes. A rather intimidating sight, she decided. Especially since it was obvious that he was going to stand right there until he got an answer.

"Just asking," she said mildly, taking a sip of tea and hoping that she didn't look as rattled as she felt. It was a feeling he evoked in her all too easily, she thought crankily.

"Feel like trusting me on this one?"

Sighing with relief when he finally turned and led the way back to the living room, she said pleasantly, "I think I'd rather look at the tapes myself, if you don't mind."

Unaware of his thoughtful gaze, she glanced curiously around the room. He had taken her through it so quickly, she had hardly gotten a chance to look around. The house itself was well built and attractive. That came as no surprise to her, after having seen the lodge and her cabin. Dave McGraw was a man who would demand, and receive, quality work for his money. The ceiling was A-line with open beams, and the walls were paneled with a light wood that would make the room cheerful and inviting even on the darkest winter days. Comfort was the overriding feature, she decided. The oak-framed furniture was attractive without being forbidding. It was the kind that allowed you to kick off your shoes and curl up on it without worrying about ruining a cascading arrangement of throw pillows. The colors were a solid blend of cream and brown with a dash of spice.

Looking back at the dining room, she commented, "It seems a bit large for one person."

"Yeah, it was built for a family," he admitted, pulling out a drawer full of tapes. "Come take a look at these and pick your poison."

A family? Ignoring the lure of that bit of news, she walked over and stood beside him. Glancing down, she gave a soft whistle after reading the titles. "You weren't kidding about poison," she said, looking up from a connoisseur's collection of mysteries and suspense thrillers.

Dave shrugged. "I like a challenge." When her eyes narrowed, his mustache twitched. "I don't like things that are too obvious, or that come too easily. I want something out of the ordinary."

"Which ones haven't you seen?" she asked, wondering suspiciously if he was being deliberately provocative or was really talking about a film.

"The first three."

"Good." She pounced and held one out to him. "I missed this when it first came out."

He slid the tape into the VCR and punched a couple of buttons while Jennifer looked around. The couch was the obvious place to sit for viewing, but any of the chairs would be safer, she thought. Dave didn't give her time to worry about it, though. While the usual ominous warning against copying the tape flashed on the screen, he led her over to the couch. Nudging a footstool closer, he kicked off his loafers, indicated that she could do the same with her sandals and had them settled before the title appeared.

Jennifer blinked at the screen, missing the entire parade of credits and the first few minutes of the story. She hadn't expected to sit quite so close to him. No, she decided thoughtfully, what she hadn't expected was being plastered against him from her ankles on up, with her bare feet cozily touching his stockinged ones on the ottoman and her head resting in the hollow of his shoulder. She felt every breath he took. And his hand cupping her hip was like a burning brand.

Part of her mind followed the complex progression of the film, while the rest catalogued everything about him. His body was hard from physical labor. When he sighed and settled deeper into the couch, taking her right along with him, the flexing muscles of his arm and chest reminded her of some superbly conditioned animal. Heat flowed out of him and into her until she couldn't tell where she ended and he began.

She hadn't been so aware of a man's body in years, she thought distractedly. Nor of her own. Every time she breathed, she pressed closer to him, and she could feel the blood pumping through her body, settling, for some unknown reason, in her head. Its roar blended with the distant rumble of thunder. Her hands seemed to be a problem, too. They were getting larger with each passing second, and she didn't know what to do with them.

Dave solved part of that difficulty by reaching over and taking her glass. After setting it on the floor between them, he grasped her wrist and ran her hand down his thigh, allowing the moisture left from the glass to be absorbed by his jeans. When that was done to his satisfaction, he shifted his hand over hers, holding it in place. She looked up and he shrugged, satisfaction gleaming in his eyes when the movement caused her cheek to settle against him and her lips to touch his throat.

His fingers flexed on her hip when she jumped and tried to back away. "Relax," he muttered. "Watch the movie."

Watch the *movie*? When her hand was being pressed close to where no woman ventures unless she's inviting trouble? When her fingers were curved on his inner thigh, and now that he had shifted a bit, the tips were caught lightly between his legs? And the heat blasting out of him was zinging through her veins?

Jennifer glanced down and let out a small sigh of relief. It really wasn't *that* bad, she told herself. Actually, her hand was only about six or seven inches above his knee, a long way from...trouble.

After a quick, sideways glance, this time at his face, she relaxed a bit more. He didn't look like a study in uncontrolled lust. As a matter of fact, he was watching the film with every indication of enjoyment. The rat.

It was just that he was so casual about the whole thing. That's what rankled. He was obviously a toucher, comfortable with his own body and assuming that everyone else felt the same way. Which, of course, was just not so. She could attest to that. If she had ever taken that same uncomplicated pleasure in touching, it was gone. Richard hadn't known the meaning of the word spontaneity. As a matter of fact, she had once scrutinized his detailed calendar to see if he blocked out time for making love.

Nothing in the years spent with Richard had prepared her to cope with a man like Dave McGraw. The ranch and all its employees, everything about him, reflected his prowling energy, his interest in the smallest detail. And he enjoyed life, took great pleasure in the tiniest things, while somewhere along the way, she had become mired in responsibility and duty. She was still brooding over that dreary realization when the movie ended.

Dave's hand tightened on her hip for a moment, then he got up and punched the rewind button. "What's the verdict?"

"It was good," she said brightly. Well, what she remembered had been well done. "Very good."

"I don't know. I thought the part where he got shanghaied by aliens was stretching it a bit far."

She looked at him in astonishment. "What?"

"You weren't even watching it," Dave said calmly, removing the tape and slipping it back in the drawer. "You were too busy wondering when I was going to jump your bones."

"I was not," she denied vigorously, lying through her teeth. "The thought never occurred to me." She held up her hand as though she were taking an oath. A deafening clap of thunder broke overhead and she jumped guiltily. Dave's deep rumble of laughter was a thoroughly male, thoroughly satisfied sound.

He came back and sat on the ottoman, facing her, taking her hands in his. Outside the open window, aspen leaves rustled as the wind whispered through them. His thighs brushed her calves, pressing them together. Inside, Jennifer shifted beneath his level gaze, blaming her tension on the impending rain.

"I want you," he said simply.

Jennifer blinked. She had been expecting something, but not this. Not words that were so simple, so direct.

"I want a lot of things," she finally answered, tugging in a futile effort to release her hands. "But I know I'll never get many of them."

"I'm not asking you to say or do anything," he continued as if she hadn't spoken. "I'm just laying my cards on the table."

"Well, I wish you hadn't," she retorted, working loose and padding across the room to stand by the screen door, staring out into the dark as if her life depended on the action. "I don't play games, especially cards. I don't even know for sure what you mean when you say that you want me."

"What do you *think* I mean?"

"That you want to hold me?"

"Yes." He stood behind her, bracing one hand on the doorjamb.

"Kiss me?"

"Yes."

"Take me to bed?" she asked rashly, driven to distraction by his nearness, the heat emanating from him.

"Yes."

"Now?"

One large hand laced through her hair and cupped her head. "Yes."

"Next month?"

His thumb brushed her nape. "Yes."

"Next year?"

"Yes."

She ducked under his arm and moved restlessly around the room, examining the built-in bookcase, picking up a magazine, putting it down to touch a leafy plant. "No wonder I didn't know what you meant. Those three little words cover a lot of territory."

His dark gaze followed every nervous movement of her body. "It's not as complicated as you make it sound."

She spun around to face him, her eyes a little desperate. "Yes, it is, and it won't work. No. That's as plain as I can say it. I like you. I like being with you, but don't start making noises about wanting and having and long-term relationships. I'm only going to be here for six more weeks, for heaven's sake. We don't *have* a future together."

Dave stared across the room at her and swore silently. Honesty wasn't always the best policy, he reminded himself. He had rushed her and probably the only thing that kept her from flying out the door was the fact that he was standing right in the middle of it.

"Okay," he said with a slight shrug and started walking toward her. "Then let's try it your way. We'll talk about here. And now."

Spears of lightning forked through the sky and the lights flickered.

"This room," Dave said, moving closer with every word. "Us. A kiss."

Jennifer's mouth opened, but thunder overhead drowned out her words.

Dropping his hands on her shoulders, Dave didn't stop moving until the tips of her breasts pressed into his chest. "No complications," he promised softly, his breath warm on her cheek. "We'll keep it simple."

He framed her face in his hands and lowered his head, brushing his mouth against hers, gently, tenderly, dropping one hand to her softly rounded bottom and pulling her against him when she murmured something indistinguishable against his lips.

"What, love?" he murmured, touching the velvet of her earlobe with the tip of his tongue.

She shivered but didn't pull away. "This is crazy."

His lips settled on hers again, then lifted, touching the corner of her mouth. "Wonderful."

With her eyes still closed, Jennifer moved her hands up from his shoulders, fingers tracing his ears, then lacing through his thick hair, languidly caressing his head. "Mmm."

The soft, dazed sound was all the encouragement that Dave needed. He shaped his mouth to hers, tightening his arms when her lips parted and she leaned into the kiss with a hunger that matched his own. His hand at the back of her head wasn't necessary. She wasn't moving away. He tasted her sweetness and she met him touch for touch, stroke for stroke.

Lightning blazed across the sky, followed immediately by a crack of thunder that shook the house. The lights flickered and went out.

Minutes later, Dave reluctantly softened the kiss, slowing them both down before they blazed completely out of control. He raised his head and held Jennifer close while they both struggled for breath.

"My God," Jennifer said just seconds later, "I'm blind."

Her stunned statement, delivered with utter sincerity, broke the tension as nothing else could have. Dave's rumbling laughter exploded in the room and he swung her up in his arms, hugging her until she was sure her ribs would crack.

"We're good, honey," he choked, giving her one last squeeze and lowering her to the floor. "But I don't know if we're *that* good. The lightning knocked the lights out. It happens every now and then. They'll be back on in a little while."

"Oh." Now that her heart was settling down, she could hear the pounding rain. She moved out of his arms and walked back to the door, saying, "It's *storming* out there." And if she hadn't been clinging to him like a limpet, unconscious to everything around her, she'd have known that.

Soundlessly, Dave appeared behind her. "Yeah, it's really coming down. You might have to spend the night."

Jennifer glanced over her shoulder to meet his teasing look. "Don't count on it," she said dryly, pointing a slim finger in the direction of her cabin. "I live right over there, remember?"

"But you wouldn't want to go out in all that, would you?" A flash of lightning punctuated the question.

"A little water isn't going to hurt me."

He draped a companionable arm around her shoulders. "Just think for a minute about the other things that might be lurking around out there."

Jennifer jumped. "Like what?" she asked, and immediately knew she'd been had. She could feel satisfaction oozing out of his pores.

"Bears?" he suggested blandly.

She shook her head. "You told me they never come down in this area."

"Wolves?"

"Give me a break," she groaned.

"Rain-soaked llama dung?"

She spared a thought for her new sandals and said, "You can drive me home."

"It'd be just as quick to carry you."

She didn't know if he was serious or not, and most of the time she couldn't tell by looking at him. But one thing she knew for sure, she wasn't going to carry a heart attack around on her conscience. He wasn't going to "tote" her anywhere. "No way," she said, forcing a small laugh. "After eating Irma's cooking for a week, I wouldn't ask that of my worst enemy."

"And I'm not the enemy?"

This time, she knew he was serious. Reaching up to touch his hand, she said, "No. Never that."

"Good." His mood switched again. "Then let's go play haunted house."

She glanced sideways at him, her eyes narrowed in thought. "Is that anything like playing doctor?"

He made an amused sound that sounded like a snort. "Lady, where *do* you get these ideas about me? My sister and I used to do it in storms when we were kids."

"I think I'm too young to hear it," she told him primly, laughing at him with her eyes. She had missed this, she realized with a pang. It had been too long since she had laughed over nothing with someone special, made stupid jokes, shared simple pleasures.

He tugged her closer, fitting her against him. "All I'm suggesting is that we light some candles."

"Whew!" She ran a finger over imaginary perspiration on her brow.

"And make some coffee."

"Do ghosts do that?"

"Ours do," he said firmly, turning her toward the kitchen. "Stay close," he directed, keeping her tucked under his arm. "I don't want you getting lost."

Once they got there, he lifted her before she realized what he intended to do and set her down on a corner of the tile counter. "I don't want to step on your toes," he said, patting her thigh before he moved away. Seconds later he was lighting candles, the kind that came in glass containers. "We always keep these around for emergencies," he explained, setting one on the table and one near the stove. He brought a third over and held it out to her.

Wordlessly, Jennifer reached for it. His mood had changed yet again, and she could feel the tension building in the room. There was nothing frightening about it, she reflected, watching the tiny flame reflected in his eyes. There was just such palpable...awareness.

Dave touched her cheek with a gentle thumb, waiting for her eyes to widen. When they did, satisfaction surged through him. This time they weren't wary, they held what he would call stunned recognition. It was her first inkling, he realized, that she might not be able to waltz out of his life at the end of six weeks. He lifted a shiny strand of hair from her cheek and tucked it behind her ear. "Beautiful lady," he murmured, brushing her bottom lip with his thumb.

Jennifer blinked and he walked back to the stove. His touch was as soft as his words and she desperately needed something to break the spell. It was just too much, she thought numbly. She could hardly hold her own with him in blazing sunshine; in candlelight it was hopeless.

In the next moment, a shred of indignation came to her rescue. Was this any way for him to treat a lady who just wanted to get her life back on an even keel? No, she answered her own question, it wasn't. He really knew how to stack the deck in his favor. Dave McGraw had a barrel full of tricks and he was pulling every one of them out, one at a time as he needed them. Of course, he hadn't planned the storm, she decided fairly, trying to give him the benefit of the doubt. A little voice inside muttered that while he might not have arranged it, he sure knew how to use it when it came along!

By the time the coffee was done, the lights were back on. Dave carried a tray with the steaming cups and some of Irma's chocolate cake back to the living room. Jennifer trailed along behind him.

"I'm driving in to Dillon tomorrow," she told him. "To give a talk for a women's organization."

"Who's in charge?"

"Hmm. I can't remember her name." She dropped down on the couch and reached for her small shoulder bag. "But I've got it in here somewhere." She rummaged through a wad of notes and folded envelopes.

Dave sat down and eyed the bulging purse with fascination. "How do you ever find anything in there?" he asked with genuine curiosity. "Look, it isn't that important. It doesn't matter."

Jennifer scowled at a small scrap of paper. "Lunch on Friday," she read. "What Friday? Where? And who with?"

Never taking his eyes off the small purse, Dave murmured, "With whom."

"That's what I just said," she told him absently, staring at the ragged edges of the cryptic message. Shrugging, she crumpled the note and said, "Well, if I missed it, I hope it wasn't important." Gripping the edges of the small leather bag, she upended it on the cushion between them.

It was like pulling a cork from an upside down jug and watching the contents flood out, Dave thought, blinking at the mass of papers that streamed out. He leaned over to pick up a couple of envelopes that had slid to the floor.

"I know it's in here," Jennifer muttered. "At least it better be. Without it, I don't have the foggiest idea where to go." While she picked up the scraps one at a time and piled them in a neat stack, Dave attempted to press the creases out of the envelopes.

"Her name had something to do with a fence. I remember that much. I said something to Madge about it. It was—Pickett! Here it is, Lillian Pickett. She's just a block or so away from the college." Waving the memo, Jennifer looked up to find Dave staring fixedly at one of the envelopes.

"Who's Jennifer Matlock?"

All the animation left her face at the question. "I am." Holding her hand out for the envelope, she amended, "I mean, I was."

"Who's R. Matlock?"

She sighed. "Richard."

"Richard?"

Nodding, she said, "The man I married five years ago."

He gestured at the envelope she was stuffing back in the bag. "That's a letter from your *husband*?"

Chapter Five

Ex-husband," she reminded him.

"For how long?"

"Long enough," Jennifer said briskly, stuffing a handful of papers carelessly back into the small bag.

Dave glanced at the postmark on the envelope. "Apparently he hasn't gotten the message yet."

"That's not *my* fault." She snagged the envelope out of his hand, folded it haphazardly and added it to the last few bits and pieces she was tucking in the purse. "I've done everything I can to convince him."

"He still writes?"

Jennifer sighed in exasperation—at Richard's thickheaded conviction that she couldn't cope without him and at Dave's persistence. "Yes. Frequently."

"How frequently?"

"As often as he thinks I need his advice," she snapped. Which averaged out to two or three times a month. "He's convinced that I won't make it out in the cold, cruel world without him."

Dave reached out for her cup of coffee and handed it to her. After taking a swallow of his own, he asked, "Exactly what does he think is out there that's going to get you?"

"Bears," she said, testing the heat of her mug with the tip of her tongue. "Wolves."

"Cute." He stared at her over the rim of his cup.

She heaved another sigh. "He lets me know when the stock market fluctuates."

Dave shrugged impatiently. "So get a broker."

"I have one. He also sends me the latest gloomy statistics on women my age remarrying. He advises me not to renew my teaching credential. He—"

"Wants you back."

She considered the flat statement for several seconds, then nodded. "Yeah, that's about the size of it."

"Are you going?"

Her look was expressive. It said, "Are you kidding?" in about four different languages.

His brows rose. "Just asking."

"Richard," she said in a tone that suggested he pay attention, "is a good man. I'm a good woman. But we weren't good for each other. He needs a woman who won't consider it a sacrifice to devote her life to him, to make him the center of her universe." Jennifer put her mug on the table and looked at it thoughtfully. That wasn't a bad summation of four years, she decided. It left out any number of things, but that was her intention.

When she turned back to Dave, the waiting expression in his dark eyes told her that she had missed something. "Hmm?"

"I said, what do *you* need?"

"To be left alone," she answered promptly. "To do what I want to do without any outside interference."

His eyes narrowed at her quick answer. "Let me rephrase that. What kind of *man* do you need?"

"I don't *need* any kind. Not now, not for a long time. Maybe never." She leaned against the back of the couch and stared at him, daring him to contradict her.

Dave's expression didn't change as he eyed the defiant tilt of her chin. The hell she didn't. No woman who kissed a man the way she had kissed him a few minutes ago would settle for a life of hard work and good deeds. No woman who shimmered with heat and fire the way she had in his arms was destined to live alone for very long.

No, whether she admitted it or not, Jennifer Hale was all woman. Regardless of what she did with her life, whatever career she followed, she would truly come alive only in the arms of the right man. And he didn't mean her idiot of an ex-husband, who had managed to bungle things so badly he had finally driven her out of his life. No, when she was ready to take her head out of the sand and admit that there was more to life than work, Dave McGraw would be waiting—right in front of her where she couldn't miss him.

"Morning, Irma. I think I want to try some of your sourdough pancakes." Jennifer smiled at some of the other lodgers and selected a table by the window. "Has Aunt Tillie eaten yet?"

"Nope, she's out there." The cook stopped at Jennifer's elbow and pointed outside. "She's been there since early this morning."

Jennifer's gaze followed the direction of Irma's finger, beyond the window to a large corral where a plump, buff-colored llama was isolated. Tillie, wearing a splash of purple, was staring at it sympathetically while several other llamas wore a track in the ground, pacing back and forth along the fence.

When Tillie looked up and waved, Jennifer raised her hand in acknowledgement, then leaned back in her chair and smiled up at Irma. "How goes the cholesterol war?"

Irma snorted. "It's winning. I've never seen a more stubborn man in all my life. He ordered eggs and crisp bacon this morning. And biscuits." She slapped down a napkin and some silverware on the table. "Were you all right last night when the lights went out?" she demanded in a quick change of subject. "Did anyone show you where the candles were kept?"

Jennifer blinked away the memory of the leaping flame reflected in Dave's dark eyes. "Yes, thanks," she said finally. "I did just fine." Tillie opened the front door, and Jennifer breathed a sigh of relief. Last night had been a definite error in judgment, and the sooner she put it out of her mind, the better off she'd be.

Irma took Tillie's order of toast and tea and trudged flat-footedly back to the kitchen.

"Men are most peculiar creatures," Tillie murmured almost to herself as she unfolded her napkin and arranged it neatly in her lap. When that was done to her satisfaction, she fished a purple purse out of her layers of fabric and withdrew an orange.

Jennifer looked up in surprise. "Why do you say that? Not that I'm arguing. I'm just curious."

A little frown pulled Aunt Tillie's silver brows closer together. "Actually, Maybelle said it. I'm just repeating it."

Maybelle? Jennifer mentally ran a quick inventory of the female members of the staff. Two college girls, Mary and Susan, who helped with the housekeeping, and Irma. Those three were the only ones she knew of.

"It came up when we were discussing how men ran things," Tillie said vaguely, peeling the orange with military precision.

"Things?"

Tillie waved her hand in a gesture that said everything and nothing. "The world. The government. The ranch. Things."

"Was there anything in particular that, uh, Maybelle is concerned about?"

Tillie's nod was brisk. "Absolutely. She doesn't like the way they're treating poor Amaryllis and the others."

Jennifer blinked questioningly. Find the right thread and it will all make sense, she reminded herself after a moment.

"Who's Amaryllis?"

Tillie tapped her finger on the windowpane, pointing. "That one. In the corral."

"The llama?"

Tillie nodded. "She's pregnant. Going to have a baby any time now."

"Ah." One down, one to go. "What others?"

"Them." Tillie pointed again, this time at the ever-increasing number of llamas pacing along the fence, betraying their agitation with jerky head movements and a rapid, choppy trot.

Returning her attention to the corral, Jennifer stared out at the lone, pacing animal and said, "She looks all right to me."

"They've done it all wrong," Tillie told her, shaking her head from side to side.

"The llamas?"

"The men." Tillie carefully broke the orange in half, removed one plump section and popped it in her mouth. "They shouldn't have separated Amaryllis from the others."

Jennifer waited until Irma slid a steaming stack of pancakes in front of her and left before she said, "I'll bite. What *should* they have done?"

"Maybelle said that they're all supposed to stay together."

"The men?"

"The llamas."

Calories or not, she was going to eat every bit of the pancakes, Jennifer decided, taking another bite. She needed the energy to cope with this conversation. "Why? Do the females act as midwives?"

"No, as protectors."

"Doesn't look to me like she needs any protection."

With a look of mild exasperation, Tillie said, "That's not the point."

"I'm sorry, Aunt Tillie, but you've lost me. What *is* the point?"

"That it's a genetic—or is it instinctive?—necessity that the females play their part. Maybelle said that all the other females are supposed to surround the mother at birthing time. They form a tight circle, facing outward, so they can fight off any predators who attack while she's delivering the baby."

"What a wonderful idea. Efficient, too."

"And the men, by separating them, are preventing them from assuming their proper roles."

"I see."

"And do you also see," Tillie said gently, "why we have to go open the gate and let the other females join Amaryllis?"

"What?" Jennifer choked on the last bite of pancake. Tillie reached across the table, an edge of purple lace at her elbow dipping into a dab of syrup, and patted her on the back.

"Shh," she whispered, giving a final light tap. "I don't think we ought to let everyone know what we're planning."

"We aren't planning anything," Jennifer said firmly. "Aunt Tillie, I was working in my cabin when Nick started separating Amaryllis from the other, uh, ladies. She didn't want to go—"

"Exactly." Tillie gazed at her expectantly. "Didn't I just tell you why?"

"And it took him a long time to do it. I don't think he'd be thrilled if we undid all his work. And, presumably, Dave gave him orders to do it, which means that Dave wouldn't like it, either!"

Tillie made a noise that sounded like, "Tcha!"

"It's just not a good idea," Jennifer finished weakly.

"Men obviously don't understand about in-
stincts—or is it genes?"

Jennifer stared across the table at the small woman.
She was tiny, but there was more than a hint of steel in
her. And she had the persistence of a bulldog.

"Maybe no one ever explained it to them," she said
slowly, picking up speed as she thought her way
through the situation. "I didn't know about it until
you told me. Why don't you just have Maybelle go
talk to Dave?"

"No." Tillie shook her head slowly, a peculiar
expression crossing her face. "I ... ah ... no. I don't
think it would work."

"Why not? It's a perfect solution. Dave's a reason-
able man. He'd listen to her."

Tillie stared pensively out the window. "I don't
think that they speak the same language."

"I'm pretty good at Spanish. Will that help?"

"I doubt it."

"Well, do you think I could understand her?"

Sighing, Tillie said, "I don't know."

"Look, why don't we try? If I can, then I could re-
lay the message to Dave." Jennifer moved her chair
back and started to rise. "Let's go find her."

Tillie's small hand touched her wrist. "We won't
have to go far," she said, looking out of the window.

"She's out there?"

"Um-hmm."

Jennifer looked out, then stood and leaned closer.
All she could see were a dozen llamas doing sentry
duty. "Where?"

"There." Tillie pointed. "The brown one with the
white legs and neck."

"White legs?" Jennifer turned her head and looked at the older woman, hoping that she had misunderstood. What she saw in Tillie's bright blue eyes convinced her that she hadn't.

"Are you telling me that Maybelle is a *llama*?" The last word came about as a breathy exhalation.

"Shh!" Tillie looked around at the other tables. "Not so loud. Of course she is."

"And you—" Jennifer's voice dropped even lower "—*talk* to her?"

Their eyes met and held for a long moment before Tillie murmured, "Not in actual words."

Jennifer stared, fascinated. "Not in—exactly how *do* you do it?"

Tillie thought for a second. "It's more telepathic than anything."

Rubbing her index finger over a knot of nerves forming between her brows, Jennifer mumbled, "I think I'm getting a headache."

"Have you had your eyes checked lately?" Tillie asked solicitously. "My niece had that problem, and all she needed was reading glasses."

"I have a pair already, thank you. Aunt Tillie," Jennifer asked, leaning closer, "are you telling me that you talk to animals?"

A beatific look crossed the older woman's face as she nodded. "In the past," she confided, "every now and then I would get these thoughts that came out of nowhere, and I would wonder. Once, while I was visiting my neighbor, it happened, and when I looked up, the cockatoo was staring at me, looking like it was waiting for an answer. Another time, it was a squirrel in the park. But *this* time," she said in a gratified voice, "there's no mistake."

"How did it happen?"

Tillie took another look around and hitched her chair closer to the table. "My meditation," she whispered.

Jennifer blinked, unable to think of one, single, solitary response to that.

Tillie nodded. "Of course, I've always meditated, you know. Just took a few minutes out of the day for some inner quiet. But, lately, I've been giving some thought to the matter and I decided that I should try something new."

"New?" Jennifer managed weakly.

Another nod. "Once, I tried it in my neighbor's hot tub, but it made me dizzy."

"Hot tub," Jennifer repeated numbly.

"Another time, I tried hanging upside down like a bat on one of those horizontal bars, but I slipped and bruised my elbow. So I decided to try it just sitting in a chair, chanting a mantra, but I'd never had one and I couldn't think of a word or phrase that I wanted to say over and over again." Blue eyes stared at her earnestly. "They all sounded very dull."

Dull. Jennifer looked at the animated woman and wondered if there had ever been a dull minute in her life. She talked to a husband who had died a dozen years ago, she predicted the future, and now she apparently had long, philosophical conversations with animals. Dull?

"So I decided that humming might be interesting."

Jennifer thought of the contented sound the llamas made and began to see a pinprick of light at the end of the tunnel.

"But I didn't know what note to hum." Tillie sighed. "All these decisions were making it very complicated. So I decided to be systematic. I'd hum *do* the first day, *re* the second, *mi* the third, and so on. I thought that by the time I reached *do* again, I'd know which one was best."

"And did you?" Jennifer asked, swept along by the enthusiasm in the bright blue eyes.

"You're jumping ahead," Tillie chided. "I was up to *fa* the day I got to the ranch, and I walked around looking for a quiet place to sit, one where I wouldn't be interrupted, or bother anyone." She frowned at the memory. "It wasn't easy," she said darkly. "Everywhere I went, that little man, Mac, popped up behind a tree or a rock.

"Finally, I found a large, smooth tree stump by the stream—where the llamas spend a couple of hours browsing every afternoon—and I sat down cross-legged and started humming *fa*."

"What happened?" Jennifer asked when Tillie stopped to put another section of orange in her mouth.

"My feet got numb."

Jennifer grinned. "No, I mean was *fa* a good note?"

"Well, it was all right," Tillie allowed, "but I still had a few more to go before I could really choose one. *Re* had been nice, too. It sort of rang around in my head. But, it was when I got to *la* that it happened."

"What did?"

"I tuned in to the llamas," Tillie said simply. "I was on their frequency or something. They moved closer and hummed at me. First one, then another, then all of them started talking at once. Maybelle—she's their leader—got them quiet and told them to take turns. They've been chattering ever since."

Jennifer leaned back and took a deep breath. No one in her right mind would believe this, she decided. People didn't tune in to animals simply by humming. If that were the case, singers all around the world would be besieged by animal communications. No, things like that just didn't happen. To normal people. To average people.

But Aunt Tillie was neither normal nor average. She apparently broke the laws of nature as easily as she tiptoed through psychic dimensions.

"What do they talk about?" Jennifer asked, genuinely curious.

Tillie's grin could have belonged to a teenager. "They're shameless gossips. Mostly they talk about themselves. Yesterday, they were telling me about the men."

Jennifer's brows rose. "Real men?"

"Llama men. There's two kinds: geldings and hunks."

"Hunks?"

Tillie shrugged. "Studs, whatever. Do you want to know about this or not?" she asked in exasperation.

"I don't want to miss a word."

"Well, every time you interrupt, I forget where I am. The geldings are males who aren't, who don't have..."

"I know what they are," Jennifer broke in again, stopping what had all the earmarks of becoming a hopelessly entangled explanation.

"They're the pack animals. They're bigger than the females and can carry more. The females are used for breeding. They're always either pregnant or nursing."

"It's obvious that they haven't heard of women's lib," Jennifer said dryly.

"They're quite happy with their lot," Tillie assured her. "After a gestation period of eleven months, they give birth to one baby and within a week they're ready to, uh, start all over."

"They *like* that?"

"For them," Tillie said firmly, "it's a good life. Maybelle said so. And it boosts their egos to know that they bring a higher price than the males. Then, of course, there are the other regular males. Maybelle had a few salacious things to say about them."

Jennifer laughed softly, thoroughly enjoying the absurd conversation. "Like what?"

"You're too young," Tillie told her with a wicked smile. "You'll get the laundered version. First of all, Jock is the male penned up in the south corral. He has, uh, fathered almost all of the young llamas on the ranch, so Dave took him away for a while to prevent too much inbreeding. The few females who haven't had . . . relations with him, will join him in the pen at the right time."

"What did Maybelle have to say about his, um, ability?" Jennifer asked delicately.

Tillie primmed her lips. "The general opinion seems to be that it's not too bad." The two women's voices joined in helpless laughter.

"What else?" Jennifer asked weakly.

"Paladin," Tillie said in a feeble voice. "He's driving them crazy by keeping his distance. Their time is divided between admiring his...assets and wondering if he's going to live up to his reputation."

"I can't stand this," Jennifer wailed, wiping away tears with her fingers. "Unbridled sex at Pine Creek."

Tillie's snort ended in a hiccup. "You never answered my question," she said in a quavery voice. "Are you going to help me open the gate for Maybelle and the other females?"

Jennifer knew she was going to say yes. She didn't want to, and knew she would regret it when Dave found out, but women had to stand together, shoulder to shoulder, even if some of them had four legs and a tail. Before she could commit herself, a young voice shrilled, "Look, a baby!"

They turned and saw a little girl glued to one of the windows. "She had a baby!"

Jennifer and Tillie looked out. The females had spaced themselves at regular intervals along the fence, facing away from the mother and child. Inside the corral, Amaryllis licked the newborn, nudging it anxiously. Within minutes, it struggled to its knees, then rose and took a few shaky steps.

By the time Dave came in, some twenty minutes later, the little one was bobbing stiffly and a bit uncertainly at its mother's side, trying to keep up when Amaryllis stepped slowly around the enclosure.

"What is it?" Jennifer asked. "Male or female?"

"I don't know," he said, dropping into the chair next to her and taking up a lot of space. "And I won't until those females move away from the fence. I can't understand them." He stared absently out the window. "They get like this every time one of them is due."

The two women exchanged a long glance, and at that moment Jennifer understood the burden carried by those who are "different." How simple it would be to explain that the llamas were cranky because he was interfering with Mother Nature's plan for them. Then, all Jennifer would have to do was explain how she came up with that fascinating bit of information. Simple. She would tell him and he would believe every word she said. Of course.

"They looked at me like they were all ready to clear their throats and let go," he added. "I'm not crazy enough to stand around and let them use me for target practice, so I thought I'd come in and have a cup of coffee."

Jennifer glanced at his empty hands, then got up and went over to the pot provided for the guests and staff. At any hour of the day the coffee was fresh, hot and strong.

Dave scowled at the mug she set between his hands. "I can carry my own cup of coffee," he told her.

Surprise widening her eyes, Jennifer sat down with a thump. "Next time, you will," she assured him.

He downed half the cup and said, "I'm sorry. You didn't deserve that. I'm a bit on edge and you just got the backlash. There's something wrong with the men, and I'll be damned if I know what it is. It's not just two or three of them, either. Every last one of them is acting strange.''

Two pairs of blue eyes communicated again, Jennifer's guilty with knowledge and Tillie's bright with satisfaction.

''What are they doing?''

Dave's gaze shifted to Jennifer. He closed one hard hand into a fist and stared at it in frustration. ''Everything. Before I can even finish telling them what needs to be done, they're doing it.''

''Most employers would feel lucky to have people like that working for them,'' she offered carefully.

''I know it. They're all hard workers, but this last week or so—hell, I don't even know when it started— they've been falling all over themselves. They're even doing *my* work.''

''Like what?''

''Like when I said I was going to check the creek for beaver dams, I went to the corral and found my horse saddled and hitched to the fence.''

''What's the matter with that?'' Jennifer asked in surprise. ''Sounds okay to me.''

''The point is, they had things to do. Other things. And we don't wait on each other around here. If I want to take my horse anywhere, I saddle it.''

Hoping to pull a smile out of him, Jennifer said, ''Well, if I were fool enough to take a horse anywhere, I'd sure be grateful if someone did the saddling for me.''

Dave's gaze sharpened. ''How grateful?''

''Very.''

''Then, lady, I can promise you—''

''Boss?''

Blinking, the determined expression slowly fading from his face, Dave turned to face Mac. "Yeah?"

Mac's boots rang on the wooden floor as he came closer. His eyes widened in astonishment as he took in Tillie's purple creation and he stopped dead in his tracks. His gaze never shifted, even when he spoke. "Nick's back with the feed. Just thought you'd want to know. And he brought back all the extra stuff Irma needed for the party."

"What party?" Tillie asked, returning Mac's glance with interest. Apparently, Jennifer thought, she hadn't seen him yet when he wasn't partially covered by rocks or trees.

"Tonight's shindig. The boss is having everyone in to—"

"Come on," Dave said, pushing his chair back with a screech and getting to his feet. "I'll help you take in the feed."

"—meet Jenny."

"Meet *me*?"

"Thanks, boss," Mac said hastily, heading for the door, "but Nick and me got the stuff put away already."

"What do you mean, meet me?" Jennifer demanded. "I didn't hear anything about it."

"Damn it, Mac," Dave yelled after the retreating hand, "it was supposed to be a surprise."

Jennifer turned a pair of steely blue eyes on the big man beside her. "Some surprise. What am I supposed to do with my hair? What am I going to *wear*?"

"It's not exactly formal," Dave said in exasperation. "A pair of clean jeans will do."

Chapter Six

I don't believe this," Jennifer groaned, even as some part of her mind admitted that she wasn't really surprised. It was, after all, a typical grab-the-bull-by-the-horns, Dave McGraw approach.

It was nine hours later, and the party was going full tilt, with well over a hundred guests. Dave had called for her at the cabin and she had been told again that a pair of clean jeans would, indeed, do. His blue Western shirt, seemed to magnify everything about him. He looked bigger, darker and hungrier than ever. In a word, she decided with a sigh, intimidating.

He had introduced her to everyone and casually mentioned her reason for being in the area. Then, just a few seconds earlier, he had left her with a murmured apology, stood on a chair to demand attention and was now telling his guests that she needed help.

"If you'll encourage her to come up here, she'll tell you all about it," he concluded.

Warm applause filled the room, and the smiling people cleared a path from Jennifer to the chair Dave was using as a platform. Torn between gratitude for the chance to reach so many people and resentment at the high-handed methods that forcibly reminded her of her former husband, Jennifer moved forward. Dave stepped down and wrapped his big hands around her waist. Swinging her up effortlessly, he tightened his fingers before releasing her.

"Give 'em hell, honey," he whispered, then stood quietly at her side.

Steadying herself by resting her fingertips on his shoulder, she smiled at the upturned faces. "Thank you. Three of your neighbors are responsible for my presence here at the ranch. They saw one of our public service spots on television and offered to help." She introduced Madge, Judi and Francie and waited for the applause to die down.

"I'm a high-school teacher," she went on, explaining how her interest in the literacy problem had developed. "But the situation exists with people of all ages, not just youngsters. Even the most optimistic figures show that at least one out of every five Americans can't read well enough to function in today's world. They can't read directions on a bottle of medicine, they don't know about health care, they can't understand written signs on the road.

"That means that your baby-sitter—" she looked at a young married couple "—might not be able to read your instructions for child care. That your employee," she spoke to a man she knew to be a wealthy rancher, "might not be able to tell the difference between liquid fertilizer and poison. And that one of your drivers," she told the owner of a store, "might be hours late with a delivery because he can't read a map. We're not talking about statistics, we're talking about people, and the problem hits closer to home than we realize."

For the next few minutes she discussed the various volunteer organizations that were fighting the spreading problem and the methods they used to train volunteer tutors. "You don't need teaching experience to be a tutor," she stressed. "The only prerequisite is that you want to help. If you can read, you can be a tutor. It's that simple."

Dave's shoulder moved beneath her fingers. "What kind of help do you need?" he prompted.

Jennifer raised her eyes to the ceiling and sighed while a ripple of amusement worked its way around the room. "I'm getting to that," she assured him dryly.

"We need tutors. If you'll volunteer, I'll train you. We need a place to hold the training sessions." Ignoring Dave's sudden movement, she went on, "We need publicity, and after we get things rolling, we'll need students. The fact that we've established a literacy council will have to be spread by word of mouth, because the people who need the help won't be able to read signs or notices in the paper." She looked around at the thoughtful crowd. "I'll be happy to answer any questions."

Fifteen minutes later, Dave's hands once again settled at her waist. He waited until her toes touched the floor before murmuring, "You knocked them dead. I knew you would."

Linking her fingers through his, she looked at him through narrowed eyes and said, "I want to talk to you."

His brows shot up at the edge in her voice. Quietly, he led her across the room, promising several people along the way that he'd bring her back to them. He opened a door and waved her into Irma's office. She walked in and turned to face him, folding her arms tightly across her chest, ignoring the tension that shivered between them. She had a bone to pick with him and she wasn't going to let the fact that he was the sexiest damn man she'd ever encountered stop her!

After closing the door behind them, he thoughtfully fingered his mustache. "I have the feeling that I just stepped on toes that were already tender from idiot Richard's combat boots."

"A perceptive man," she stated dryly. "Too bad you didn't think of that before you did it."

"Exactly what am I being accused of? What did I do?"

"This." Jennifer flung an arm in the direction of the people they'd left behind. "The party."

Dave settled his shoulders against the wall and examined her stubborn expression. "You have some problem with accepting help?"

"I have a big problem with not being consulted." Her eyes shot sparks of blue fire.

"You don't like surprises?"

"They're fine in their place."

"Exactly where is that?"

"Anywhere outside of, and separate from, my job."

"Why is that?" His eyes softened as he took in the defensive tilt to her chin.

The adrenaline surging through Jennifer's body had prepared her for battle, not tenderness or understanding. While she could have stood toe-to-toe with him over the issues of control and interference, she knew that she had no defense against kindness. If that's what it really was.

"Why did you do it?" she countered.

He shrugged irritably. "You wanted to meet people. They're my neighbors; it was no big deal to throw a party. You need volunteers. These are the people who would be most likely to come forward, anyway."

She waited, but apparently he had said all he intended to. "That's it?"

He nodded. "That's it. It's that simple," he said, repeating the words she had said earlier.

Jennifer blinked. Was it really? When Richard had come down on her like an avalanche, putting a stop to one thing or another, he invariably had an ulterior motive. It had always been because it would take up too much time or it wasn't an "appropriate" involvement for the wife of a man in his position.

"I answered your question," he reminded her, watching every fleeting expression on her face. "I'd like to know why this bothers you so much."

"Partly because I had to put up with a lot of heavy-handed interference in the past," she grudgingly admitted. "Aside from that, I simply like things to be organized efficiently. I can't plan if I don't know what's already been done and what hasn't."

"Hmm."

"How would you like it if you were arranging a work schedule for tomorrow, and each time you mentioned a task, I said that it had already been done?"

He grinned. "I'd love it."

"Maybe. And maybe you'd be a little resentful because I hadn't discussed the matter with you."

"Maybe," he allowed. "Is that the whole point? You want to be consulted?"

"And I want final approval," she said firmly, thinking that if she gave Dave McGraw a foot, he'd probably assume that he could take an acre.

He moved away from the wall and gestured toward the door. "In that case, you'd better come and take a look at something."

"What?" Her eyes narrowed suspiciously. If ever a man looked like he was up to his ears in intrigue, this was the one.

"You'll see," he hedged. "As long as you're already mad, we might as well get this over with."

"Dave." It was a warning, pure and simple.

"Come on." He dropped a hand on her shoulder and nudged her toward the door. "Call it an exercise in conservation. It'll keep you from getting upset all over again." He kept talking as he led her out the back way and across the grassy incline.

"Why don't I find that comforting?" she muttered, hanging on to his arm, aware of the anticipation that was flowing through him. She found herself hoping that she would share his excitement. He was taking great pleasure in leading her to wherever it was they were going, and with a mild sense of shock she realized that she didn't want him to be disappointed. "Just where are we going?" she asked a minute later.

"A little farther. Watch where you're stepping," he warned, diverting her attention to the matter of unconfined llamas and the unpleasant souvenirs they left behind for those who walked without a wary eye on the ground.

"Almost there." He fished in his pocket for a key and brought her up to one of the cabins. "Okay, stand right there. Don't move. Close your eyes until I tell you to open them."

"Dave."

"Shh. I'm concentrating." His only response to her audible sigh was a chuckle. "Patience is a virtue that you obviously need to cultivate. Almost ready." He opened the door, flipped on the light and led her into the room. "Watch your step. Stop. All right, now."

Jennifer opened her eyes, squinting in the bright light. Then the shock of what she was seeing made her forget about the assault on her eyes. "You've made it into a classroom! When did you—"

"I didn't," he answered with a touch of irritation. "I told Nick how I wanted the place to look, and before I knew it, it was all done. I didn't even get to carry in a chair."

The room was ideal. The original furniture had been removed and in its place, long tables and comfortable chairs had been brought in for the students. A smaller table along the wall was perfect for books and material. Several of her alphabet charts hung from the front wall and an easel held her large flip cards.

"There's even a lectern!" She took a quick turn around the room and came to a stop behind the walnut stand. Running her hand along the smooth wood, she looked up just in time to catch the flash of pleasure in Dave's eyes. "There's room for at least twenty people in here. You think big, don't you?"

He shrugged. "Why not?"

Resting her elbows on the lectern, Jennifer leaned forward. "Why, Dave? Why did you do it?"

He looked around the room, then back at her glowing face. "You needed a place. I had one."

"Just that simple," she said softly.

Dave nudged the corner of a table with his thigh until it lined up with its neighbor. "That's right."

"But you rent these cabins. You'll be losing money on this one."

"There's never been a time when all of the rooms in the lodge and all the cabins were rented at the same time. It's no big deal."

"It is to me. Thank you."

"It's my pleasure." His voice was as soft as hers. Seconds later, just to remove her sudden pensive expression, he prodded a bit. "You're not mad?"

The corners of her mouth curled. "I would have been tomorrow. It's a good thing you caught me when I was weak."

He nodded. "Yeah, well, I decided that I'd better get you when you had already stretched being mad as far as it would go."

"Dave," she began cautiously, "I do love the room, you know that. But do you understand that I'm serious about this? That I need to be in charge, know what's going on, and make the decisions?"

"Be in charge of what?" he asked curiously.

"My life," she answered, realizing that he was asking more than he put into words. "My work, my leisure, my hobbies, my interests. I simply want to succeed or fail on my own, to make my own choices, to be left alone to make those choices. And I'll extend the same courtesy to everyone else. I'm not trying to run you or anyone else in the world."

He tilted his head, watching her expression, knowing that she was in the grip of some unpleasant memories and wishing that he could land the toe of his boot on the backside of her blockhead of an ex-husband.

"Well, it doesn't sound too hard," he decided, hungry for the sight of her smile. "But I have this problem, and it just breaks out every now and then. I'll try to keep a lid on it, but if I feel it getting the best of me, I'll be sure to let you know."

Jennifer eyed him sternly. He was too big and too tough to have this streak of playfulness, she thought, trying to discipline the smile tugging at the corners of her mouth. He fell into the role of the laid-back cowboy so naturally, it was obvious he'd had years of practice. "Does your, uh, problem have a name?" she asked politely.

He touched his mustache. "Different people call it different things. Irma says it's damned nosiness. Nick—though he's still young enough to think I might fire him if he's too honest—says I have a tendency to get involved in the affairs of people I like. Now Mac just says I'm too interfering for my own good."

"So the next time you put your nose where it isn't wanted, I'm supposed to remember that it's because you like me?"

Dave's slow stride was deceptive. It ate up the distance between them and he reached Jennifer long before she thought he would. "Yeah, honey." His hands framed her face and held it still for his kiss. "Remember that I like you—a lot." He didn't let go of her immediately, instead savoring her startled expression, the way her eyes widened, then closed, the deep breath that shuddered through her, pressing her soft body deeper into his.

"I think we'd better get back to the party," Jennifer said, wincing at the breathless quality of her voice. He was getting to her. In spite of all her resolutions when she left Richard and the "get-tough" policy she'd established, he was getting to her.

She was crazy, she decided, walking back to the lodge in silence, hardly aware of his arm draped across her shoulders. This was a man who got his way by hook or crook. If he didn't get it by a head-on confrontation, he did it by blatant application of charm. His approach was a far cry from Richard's, but the results were the same. He got exactly what he wanted, when he wanted. But Plan B had been devised for just this kind of man—and that, of course, was running, not walking, to the nearest exit!

Music and voices spilled out into the night air as they approached the lodge. They were caught up in the cheerful clamor as soon as they entered the room.

"Jennifer," Nick called, "I've got a couple of people over here who just can't wait to get their names on your sign-up sheet."

She looked up at Dave. "Will you excuse me for a while? Duty calls."

His fingers flexed at her waist and held her close for a moment. "That's what tonight is for," he said calmly. "You make the rounds, look them over, hang on to the keepers and toss the rest back in the water."

"Hush," she begged, laughing up at him. "Let's be a little more subtle about it."

"Call it what you want, that's the way you get the job done."

"I'll do it my way, thank you," she said sedately, blinking at his sexy grin.

In a lazy voice, he asked, "And how's that?"

"By hanging on to the keepers and tossing the rest back."

"Now why didn't I think of that?" he wondered aloud, sliding one big hand down until it shaped her soft bottom. Giving her a slight nudge, he reminded her, "Time's a-wasting. Better get to work."

Several hours later, before the last of the guests were out the door, Nick and some of the hands were helping Irma straighten up the room. Dave was talking to a neighbor on the porch, and Jennifer was placing her clipboard in a safe spot on one of the bookcases.

"Come on, guys, we've got to hustle. Let's get this furniture moved before the boss comes back in and starts hauling it around," Nick ordered in a quiet voice.

"This is crazy," John grunted, lifting one end of a heavy couch and sliding it back in place. "He's not dumb, you know. Every time one of us does something for him, he looks like he just smelled a dead skunk. He's going to find out sooner or later, and I'm all for it being sooner."

Nick turned an armchair around to face the fireplace. "I know. I told Aunt Tillie the same thing. If there's anything wrong with him, he needs to check in with a cardiologist. Besides, it's taking years off of my life just trying to keep one jump ahead of him."

"Okay, Len," Dave called. "I'll drop by next week. See you."

"Hustle, guys," Nick hissed.

Dave walked in and found Jennifer struggling with a square end table that was proving to be unexpectedly heavy. "Hey, you shouldn't be hauling the furniture around," he told her with a frown, clamping his hands on the sides of the table. "There's enough of us here to do it."

Nick eased in and plucked the table from between them. "I told Jennifer I'd move it."

"Why don't you start picking up the glasses?" Dave asked her, putting his hand on the back of an upholstered chair.

"'Scuse me, boss," John mumbled, "gotta slide this chair over here."

"Yeah," Dave repeated, staring blankly at a hand that was now hanging in midair, "you get the glasses and I'll move this last table."

"I got it, boss!" Two voices rang out at the same time as John and Nick jumped for the table. Either one of them could have hefted it with one hand, but they took one look at Dave's frown and, working as a team, settled it next to a large upholstered chair.

"What the hell is—"

"Dave," Irma interrupted, "these lunkheads have some of this stuff in the wrong place. Why don't you show Jennifer how to use the dishwasher, and I'll supervise in here?"

"I can help out here," he told her.

"Nope." She shook her head stubbornly. "I'll be the brains this time. You'll be more useful in the kitchen."

Fortunately, Jennifer thought as Dave stepped back so she could lead the way to the kitchen, he didn't have an image problem. He was almost as willing to tackle the mess in the kitchen as he was to flex his muscles in the living room. Almost. But his reluctance had nothing to do with the work involved, she mused, noting his preoccupied frown as she rinsed dishes and he stacked them in the washer.

In an effort to divert his thoughts, she commented, "I didn't see Mac tonight."

"No, he's not big on social events. He's got a poker game going in the bunkhouse."

"He's big on poker?"

"I don't know one old-time cowboy who isn't. If he was marooned on a desert island, he'd find somebody to cut the deck."

"Night, boss. Night, Jennifer." Nick and John ducked their heads in the doorway.

Jennifer looked up with a smile. "Night, guys."

Dave grunted and stared at them with a thoughtful frown.

"Hand me those trays, please," Jennifer said hastily, pointing behind him to the stove. As he reached for them, the two young men slipped away.

A few minutes later, Jennifer looked around at the gleaming sink and counters with satisfaction. "Done," she announced. Dave switched on the dishwasher and they left it humming in the darkened room.

A few guests were gathered around the fireplace, talking quietly, and there was a cheerful hubbub around the bar. "Wait here a minute," Dave told her.

A few seconds later, he appeared with a bottle of wine. "Your place or mine?" he asked with raised brows.

"Mine," she said promptly, hoping that it would be easier to send him home than it had been to leave his place the other night. "But, first I have something I promised to leave with Aunt Tillie." She picked up her clipboard and tugged at an envelope. "It's a list of literacy councils that she wanted to take home with her."

"Is she planning to become a tutor?"

"I don't know. Maybe she's going to tell all her relatives that Walter says they should get involved in the program."

"That'll do it," he agreed, opening the hall door. "All she has to do is bring him into the conversation, and she's got everyone jumping." He stopped at the last door and tapped gently. "Aunt Tillie?"

"Do you suppose she's sleeping?" Jennifer whispered.

Dave shrugged. "Was she expecting you?"

"I thought so. Not that there's any hurry about getting the list to her, but I had it and she didn't have any pockets in her outfit, so she said to bring it down before I left."

Dave's mustache twitched. "Outfit? That's diplomatic. What *was* that thing she was wearing?"

"I don't know. It looked like material from a hot-air balloon, gathered at the waist with an elastic belt. Do you suppose she's all right?" she asked worriedly.

Dave knocked again, a little louder.

"I don't like this," Jennifer told him after a short pause. "She could have fallen down or—what are you doing?" she asked, watching him pull out his wallet.

"Master key," he said succinctly. "I always keep one for emergencies." He opened the door soundlessly and turned on the light. "Stay here," he ordered. "I'll look around."

Too concerned to wait, Jennifer followed him in and peeked into the bathroom. "No one in here," she announced. They both looked around the room. The bed was made and nothing had been disturbed. Tillie was nowhere in sight.

"Where do you suppose she is?"

Dave shook his head. "I don't know. She wasn't in the TV room watching one of those science fiction things she's addicted to."

"She wasn't reading in the lounge, either. What else does she like to do? It's too late now to go out and gossip with the llamas," Jennifer said absently.

"Gossip?" Dave asked in a strangled voice, turning away from the closet.

Smiling weakly, she said, "A poor choice of words. I meant visit. *Think*," she ordered. "Where else could she be?"

"The only other thing I know she likes to do is play..." Their eyes met and Dave's voice dwindled away.

"Cards!"

"Mac."

"The bunkhouse! Let's go!"

A few minutes later, Jennifer's first thought was that if any of Zane Grey's cowboys had seen this bunkhouse, they would have thought they'd died and gone to heaven. Upstairs, Dave explained, each of the men had his own room. Downstairs was a small kitchen with a microwave oven, which had been put in to keep the men from making a mess of Irma's kitchen after she had cleaned it up for the evening. Next door was a TV room with a VCR and drawers full of tapes. Beyond that, claiming most of the floor space, was a lounge with comfortable chairs and a couple of couches.

In the far corner was a large, round game table. Every chair was occupied, and if the silence in the room was any indication, the play was intense. Jennifer came to a sudden stop in the doorway, entranced. The men at the table, regardless of size, had been toughened by hard work and weather, and in their boots, jeans and sturdy work shirts, they merely emphasized the femininity of the small, silver-haired woman next to them. Jennifer knew that she would never forget the scene before her.

"Hit me," ordered Aunt Tillie.

Mac glared at her, his fringe of hair bristling in outrage. "Damn it, Miss Tillie, you ain't even looked at your card."

"Hit me."

"There oughtta be some rule that says you have to look at your cards," he grumbled.

"Hit her!" chorused the men.

Muttering beneath his breath, Mac flipped a card and it skidded to a stop next to Tillie's other two. She slowly turned over the bottom card.

"Blackjack." Two small hands neatly scooped the pot from the center of the table.

Dave put his hand on the small of Jennifer's back and urged her over to the table. "Hustling again, Aunt Tillie?" he asked pleasantly.

"Just matchsticks, David." Her sedate answer was spoiled by an impish grin.

Two of the hands jumped up and said together, "Here, boss, have a seat."

Dave stared at them grimly, then sighed and took a chair. He raised his brows at Jennifer and patted his thigh in invitation. A bit pink in the cheeks, she stepped closer and perched tentatively on the offered seat.

"Miss Tillie here," Mac said, scowling at the placid woman, "wanted to learn how to play blackjack."

"So you taught her." Dave's hand tightened in warning on Jennifer's waist when her lips parted.

"Now, David, don't be upset." Tillie's blue eyes sparkled. "I knew how it said to do it in the book, but I'd never played the game with cards. So I came over here and these boys were nice enough to show me. I made sure that we didn't bet real money, though."

Mac stared at her searchingly. "How did you know we were having a game?"

Tillie avoided looking at Dave and Jennifer. "Someone must have told me," she murmured vaguely. "Do I get to deal now?"

"No!" All of the men spoke at once.

"Why not?" Jennifer demanded, suspecting that just a tad of male chauvinism was floating around.

"Because," Mac said frankly, "she don't know the first thing about dealing. If we ask for a card and she don't think we should take it, she sits there shaking her head and clucking her tongue at us."

Dave's mustache twitched, and Jennifer felt the tremor that ran through his body.

"It's true, boss, so help me," Nick said with a broad smile.

Tillie exchanged a deeply feminine look with Jennifer. She moved her hands and exposed the massive pile of matchsticks before her, then she looked pointedly at the matches thinly scattered in front of the men. "I rest my case," she muttered.

Mac glared at her and slid the cards toward Nick. "Deal."

Nick shuffled dexterously and the cards flew around the table. Tillie hitched her chair back and went over to the couch to open her purse. "Hit me," she said absently, rummaging for a tissue. "Again." Her voice was muffled as she delicately sniffed and dabbed at her nose. She returned, flipped the cards and said, "Blackjack."

Mac smacked the table with a gnarled fist. "I swear to God," he said, spacing the words for emphasis, "you'd think she knows what the cards are without even looking!"

Chapter Seven

Jennifer left the small town of Wisdom and headed north, back to the Wise River area. She had taken what was rapidly becoming one of her favorite drives: a lopsided circle from the ranch south to Dillon, then northwest to Wisdom and finally back to the ranch. Dillon, she had decided on her first visit, was an interesting place. Part college town, with a central building that reminded her of an old castle, and part focal point for five rich ranching valleys. A place where students met on one side of the street and debated the latest issues, and ranchers met on the other, discussing the age-old problems of weather, crops and livestock.

The first time she had made the drive had merely reinforced her impression that Montana was composed of a series of mountain-rimmed valleys linked together under an umbrella with the appropriate name of Big Sky. It was definitely a sky with character, she mused, at least when compared to Southern California's customary smog-tinged blueness. Here, it was rarely the same for two days running. So far, in the short time she had been here, it had ranged from a clear, vivid blue to a murky gray and from a dramatic show of white, puffy clouds to an even more theatrical display of dark ones broken by jagged forks of lightning.

She swung the Buick to the right, onto the dirt road that led back to the ranch. She knew from experience that before she got there she would undoubtedly be stopped by cows on the road, that she would spot a deer or two and that she would have plenty of time for thought. The first two points she didn't mind; it was the last one that was the killer.

Mainly because it wasn't getting her anywhere. She had expended more brainpower on a man in the three weeks that she had been on Dave McGraw's ranch than she had done in the entire four years she'd been with Richard—and with fewer results. He was purely and simply driving her crazy.

First of all, there was her physical reaction to him. Her body reacted like a hot-blooded adolescent every time he came near her. It paid absolutely no attention to the warnings to proceed cautiously that her head was giving her. Then, it was hard to keep her distance from a man who might be extremely ill. Grim as it sounded, the possibility had to be faced. If Aunt Tillie had understood the message from the great beyond correctly, Dave could be in serious trouble. The fact that he didn't look as if he'd ever been sick simply made it more confusing. And he acted like a man who took superb health for granted. All of which had caused some interesting reactions when she had advised him not to carry in bags of groceries or asked him if he wanted to rest when they walked around the ranch.

If he had turned out to be one-dimensional and easy to categorize, she wouldn't have a problem, either. She would have been able to dismiss him with no regret and get on with her job. But he was liked and respected by everyone she met. He was fair and treated his employees with the same consideration he accorded his business associates. And, while he often chose to assume the role of laconic cowboy, he was no dummy. He knew ranching backward and forward and had a college degree in business.

He was also direct, she reflected, recalling how he had simply, straightforwardly, told her that he wanted her. But he didn't push. At least, not too obviously. He was just always there—wherever she was. Prowling. Sexy. Waiting. Tacitly reminding her that nothing had changed—that he still wanted her. And being so charming that it was getting harder every day to resist him. But Richard had been charming, too. At first.

She shook her head, remembering how unsuspecting she had been. At twenty-one, she should have known better. But, she rationalized for the thousandth time, the situation had evolved slowly. It hadn't been recognizable when Richard had appeared in her life. He had been good-looking, pleasant, they'd shared a number of interests, and he had a promising future. All the requirements for a husband and father, she'd thought.

He wasn't a bad man. He had simply developed a major case of tunnel vision where his job was concerned. As time passed, it had grown even stronger. His primary concern had been that she do nothing to jeopardize his position in his archconservative law firm.

But, in his own way, he had loved her. Unfortunately, his way had been to clip her wings and put her in a cage, one with bars that periodically drew closer, smothering and finally extinguishing the last remnants of joy in her life. It hadn't helped that her brand of love had been no wiser. For some unknown reason, she had accepted the sole responsibility for making their marriage work. Even as things had grown increasingly worse, she had believed that if she went the extra mile, gave just a little more, the marriage would be saved. So she had given. Given *up* was a more accurate description, she reflected. First her friends, then her job. That had been followed by her sense of humor, her expectations, and finally—four years later, when she realized that the price was simply too high—her husband.

She knew now that she had set herself an impossible task. Marriage was a two-way street, far more than a fifty-fifty proposition. Each partner, at different times, had to be willing to give the entire hundred percent.

Such wisdom, she thought wryly, hanging on to the steering wheel as she turned the car in a serpentine pattern to avoid a series of holes in the road. Too bad it had come so late. The disaster of her marriage had left her, if not a sadder, definitely a wiser woman. And a wary one. If she ever contemplated taking that step again—and that was a big "if"—it would be only after a lot of thinking and even more plain talking. She would want to know how this unnamed and unspecific male, who looked nothing at all like Dave, she assured herself, felt toward the woman in his life. Would he grant her the same independence of thought and freedom of action that he expected for himself? Nothing less would satisfy her now.

Slowing to a stop and honking at a couple of cows that were standing in the middle of the road regarding her with interest, she had a sudden thought. Just suppose that she were looking for such a man. Would Dave McGraw fit the bill? Acknowledging the way her body reacted when she was within a country mile of him, she admitted that in some ways, he would. But when she remembered last week's party and the cabin that had magically become a classroom, only two examples of his recent actions, she had doubts. True, his behavior could be labeled as supportive; it could also be called interference.

Jennifer sighed at the next doubt that clamored for attention. God only knew that she hated to give Richard's past actions power over her present life, but he had managed to dent her self-confidence. Sometimes she felt as if she had to prove that she was capable—if not to anyone else, then to herself. Would Dave have been as helpful to anyone involved with the literacy program? Or did he see her as incompetent, someone who couldn't cope on her own, someone who needed an outsider to step in and salvage the operation?

Jennifer, she told herself silently, *you're paranoid.*

Yes, she admitted, just as quietly, *I am. But since someone spent four years trying to do me in, I'm entitled!*

With that cheerful thought ringing in her head, she pulled into the ranch yard, avoiding the pine trees with their sticky sap and parking beneath a large maple. She found Aunt Tillie sitting on the doorstep of her cabin, an abstracted expression on her face.

"This is a pleasant surprise. Have you been waiting long?"

"No, dear. Not at all." Tillie stood up, shook the wrinkles out of her bright yellow outfit and followed Jennifer into the cabin. Tillie moved around the room, touching a magazine, straightening a picture on the wall, looking at her reflection in a small mirrored clock.

"Is something wrong, Aunt Tillie?"

"No, dear, of course not." She sat down in one chair and immediately got up to try the other. "Well, perhaps. Yes."

"Ah." Jennifer nodded soberly. "That certainly clears things up. Aunt Tillie, before we get any deeper into this, I've got to know something."

"What's that, dear?" Silver brows peaked in interest.

"I like my bad news up front. Straight and to the point. Are you bringing me a message from Uncle Walter?"

Tillie blinked thoughtfully. "Now, why would I do that?"

"I don't know. I'm just trying to get geared up for the worst."

"Oh, dear. Walter's reputation is spreading," she murmured in obvious dismay.

"Aunt Tillie!"

"No, dear. No message."

Jennifer blew out a gusty sigh of relief. "Let me make some tea, and we'll talk."

"About what?"

"Whatever's on your mind," Jennifer said gently, running water into the teakettle and setting it on the burner.

The women waited silently for the water to boil, each occupied with her own thoughts. After a few minutes Jennifer put a steaming cup and a small plate of cookies on the table next to Tillie, then took a cup for herself and curled in the corner of the couch. She sipped her tea and waited patiently for Tillie to begin.

"I've enjoyed my little chats with the llamas," the older woman said finally.

"I can imagine. Have you picked up any more nuggets you care to pass on?"

Tillie smiled. "Never stand upwind of one of them who's mad enough to spit."

"Makes sense. I'll remember that. All I have to do is figure out when they're getting mad."

"One way is to watch their chins."

"Chins?" Jennifer asked, wondering if she had heard correctly.

"Chins. If they raise them as if they're looking at the sky, it means that someone—or something—is invading their space and they're warning them off. If you're around, get ready to duck."

Jennifer gazed at her admiringly. "Now that you've conquered Llamaland, what's next? Horses? Dogs?"

Tillie nibbled on the cookie. "I'm not quite ready to move on yet."

"You mean that there's a holdout? Someone's not talking?"

"Most of them are," Tillie said with a slight frown. "Even Jock, who is certainly in a vile mood. But—" she cast a woman-to-woman glance at Jennifer "—I suppose he has reason. He's angry and jealous."

"Of the new man in town, the mysterious loner, the—"

"Paladin."

Alerted by the other woman's tone of voice, Jennifer leaned forward. "Is that the one? He won't talk? At all?"

Tillie shook her head slowly, deliberately. "I sometimes wonder if he is—no, it couldn't be. There'd be no reason. But, on the other hand, I don't know what else it could be. Do you?"

"Do I what?" Jennifer asked, thoroughly confused.

"All of the others talk," Tillie murmured as if to herself. "Heavens, do they talk. They talk about the new babies and the people who go backpacking. They're still trying to figure out why Mac was peeking at them from behind the trees. And they're convinced that there's nothing wrong with David's heart."

"Really?"

Nodding, Tillie said, "That's one of the reasons I haven't told David. I don't want to alarm him if there's a chance that Walter is wrong."

I don't believe this, Jennifer thought, taking a deep breath. We're discussing the possibility of a man having a heart attack—or worse—and the only evidence we have comes from a dead man and a herd of llamas! "You've got to make a decision soon," she warned again. "He should really see a doctor."

"There is a strong possibility that matters will shortly be taken out of my hands."

"What does *that* mean?"

"I don't know."

"Aunt Tillie, I think this method of dealing with things leaves a lot to be desired."

"I've always thought so," the family psychic said dryly.

"Where were we before we got sidetracked?"

"Paladin."

"Ah." Jennifer gave some thought to the matter, then said, "If he's the only one not talking, the percentages are on your side."

"That's not what matters. I think he's doing it deliberately," Tillie said, miffed. "He's playing head games with me. When I go anywhere near him, he deliberately moves away. He won't even look at me. If I follow him, he puts some sort of a shield up."

"You mean, a psychic one? Is there such a thing?" When she got a nod of approval, she said, "Maybe it isn't that at all. Maybe he's on a different frequency or something."

Tillie shot her a sideways glance. "The others can talk with him, and I can talk with them, therefore, I should—"

"Be able to talk to him," Jennifer said in resignation.

"Exactly."

"Have you asked Maybelle about it?"

"Um-hmm."

"What does she say?"

"She's very vague. Says he has a problem. That he's trying to work through it."

"Odd. How about the others?"

"They're no more forthcoming than Maybelle."

"Does it really matter?"

Tillie looked up at that. "Yes. For some reason, I think it does. I suppose I'll just have to be patient."

Jennifer stared down at the cup she was cradling in her hand. Three weeks ago, if anyone had been interested enough to want to know, she would have said that she was a rational person, not given to flights of fancy. And if she had been asked her opinion on psychic phenomena, she would have tactfully stated that it sounded intriguing but she honestly didn't know if there were people who could predict the future.

So much for three weeks ago. Now she was sitting in her living room having a serious discussion with a "genuine, gold-plated" psychic about why a superstud llama wouldn't talk. And she was offering advice to the psychic, such as it was. It would have been different if they had been in California, which had a reputation for harboring and even nurturing "crazies." But this was Montana, a state inhabited by practical, no-nonsense people. Somehow, even that didn't dispel the credibility of the energetic, clear-eyed lady who—

"Jennifer? Are you home? Have you seen Aunt Tillie?" The voice was unmistakable, and both women gave a guilty start.

Dave appeared at the doorway in the wake of his words. There was a grim set to his features that was reflected throughout his body. For someone who was reputed to have an even disposition he had all the ear-marks of being in a nasty temper, Jennifer thought with surprise. It was a sight she could have waited indefinitely to see.

"Ah, my two favorite women," he said in a cool voice that matched the menace in his eyes. "Together. How convenient. I want to have a little talk with you."

"David, dear." Tillie jumped up. "How nice. Unfortunately, I have a most urgent—"

"Aunt Tillie, sit!" He pointed to the chair she had just left.

"Not now, David, I have something—"

"Now," he said firmly. "Sit."

She sat, sneaked a look at Jennifer, then raised her eyes to the ceiling. Dave dropped down on the couch beside Jennifer, his weight tilting her cushion downward and bringing her closer to him. She hastily wiggled back into the corner, folding her legs beneath her.

"Who wants to start?" he asked, looking from one to the other.

"Start what?" Tillie looked at him with wide-eyed innocence. It was obviously an expression that had been perfected over the years, Jennifer decided. It had a "how to get out of a tight spot when your back is against the wall" look to it. Her own expression, she thought with resignation, was probably no more convincing.

"No takers?" he asked evenly. "Then maybe I should begin."

Jennifer lifted her hand as if to touch him, then dropped it back in her lap. "Dave—"

"No." He shook his head. "I want to take a crack at it." He shifted on the sofa and stretched out his legs. "Three weeks ago, my life was predictable. I worked around here, doing the haying, building fences, whatever had to be done. I did my share right beside the rest of the men. Then—" his deliberate gaze moved from one to the other of them "—I went to Butte to pick you up at the airport. That's when everything began to change."

"David, there's—"

He held up a quelling hand. "My turn," he reminded her. "I'm thirty-four years old and lately everybody on this ranch has been acting like I'm ninety. At first, I didn't think too much about it. If anything, I thought that some of the men were hustling for a raise. But whatever's going on seems to be contagious."

Dave rose and paced over to the window. He jammed his hands into his back pockets and stared down at the stream. At the same time, he could see the two women reflected in the glass. "Whenever I ask Irma for something to eat, I have a fight on my hands. When I walk in the bunkhouse, men my own age, or older, jump up and offer me their chairs. John is going to have a heart attack—" he paused as Jennifer and Tillie visibly twitched and turned to look at each other "—running to keep ahead of me so he can open the gates. Nick is all over the place, lifting, hauling, doing half of my work."

Dave turned and leaned against the sill, staring down at Jennifer, his mouth set in a grim line. "You were upset because I lifted an armload of books the day you got here, and when we go for walks, you act like you think you might have to carry me home.''

Jennifer stared back, trying not to look as guilty as she felt. She couldn't think of a thing to say that didn't implicate the small woman beside her. And she wasn't ready to do that—yet.

With a swift movement, Dave slid the other chair forward, pushing it between the two women. He sat down and turned narrowed eyes on Tillie. ''Not ten minutes ago, I had a wrestling match with Mac down by the corral. He's a foot shorter than me, a hundred pounds lighter, and he insisted on carrying my saddle.'' Reaching out and tucking Tillie's small hand between his big ones, he said, ''You're the only one who hasn't hovered over me, and considering that all this began when you arrived, I can't help thinking that this is the hand that's been pulling the strings around here.''

''Now, David,'' she began briskly, ''you know—''

He shook his head. ''It won't work, Aunt Tillie. You could stop me cold when I was thirteen, but not now. This time, I want an answer.''

She focused on him, her bright eyes unblinking.

''You didn't come here just for a vacation, did you?'' he asked, gently squeezing her tiny hand.

Tillie sighed and looked furtively at Jennifer, whose shrug clearly said, *Don't ask me. I didn't start this mess.* Tillie turned back and was pinned by her nephew's implacable gaze. ''I told Jennifer all about it,'' she said cravenly.

Jennifer jumped when the hot potato landed in her lap. ''Oh, no, I couldn't do justice to the story,'' she blurted. ''I'll go make some more tea while you two talk." Her escape was stopped in midflight when Dave's hand closed around her wrist. His grip wasn't painful, but it was as effective as a manacle.

"No."

Short, sweet and to the point, she thought wryly, remaining right where she was. He wasn't loud, but he was very, very definite.

He kept his hand on her wrist, and his gaze brushed like a physical touch over her lips before he turned back to his aunt. "Why don't you start from the beginning," he directed.

"It was the middle of May," Tillie said obediently. "I was going out to sit in the gazebo for a while, but first I wanted to check some of my roses for thrips. Once I said good morning to my neighbor, Mr. Franks, you remember him, David—the man who plants worms? I went back to the roses—"

"Plants worms?" Jennifer choked.

Dave sighed. It was going to be a long afternoon. "Night crawlers," he said succinctly. "For fishing."

"Nasty things," Tillie went on, not even stopping for breath, "they suck the juice right out of the plants."

"I thought worms were good for plants," Jennifer said doubtfully.

Tillie blinked. "They are. You're very fortunate if you have them in your soil."

"Then what sucks—"

"Thrips," Dave said through clenched teeth.

"Nasty little things," Tillie repeated. "I check all year long to make sure they don't get a foothold."

Shifting impatiently, Dave said, "What does this have to do with you coming out here?"

"Now, David, how can I keep things straight, if you keep interrupting?"

"But—"

"You *did* ask me to start at the beginning," she reminded him. "Where was I?"

"Worms and thrips," Jennifer prompted, biting back a smile at Dave's frustrated groan.

"After I got through, I went to sit in the gazebo. It's my favorite place to go when I want to talk to Walter," she explained to Jennifer. "We talked for a long time and—" she took a quick peek at Dave "—that's when he first mentioned it."

"It?" The one word was all he allowed himself. He knew from experience that it did no earthly good to rush her when she was on a roll.

"Now, David, I don't want you to think that I didn't care. The fact that it took me six weeks to come here wasn't due to a lack of concern. You do understand, don't you?"

He nodded encouragingly, hoping that eventually he *would* understand.

"The thing was," Tillie continued earnestly, "I couldn't believe it. No—" she held up her hand as if to stop him "—I know that I shouldn't doubt Walter. He is right time and time again. But there are those exceptions, of course—" her eyes widened indignantly "—when that happens, he tells me that *I* misunderstood."

Dave leaned back and sighed. He was listening to Tillie but his gaze was moving over Jennifer in a lazy, appreciative sweep. Watching her expressive face, the humor that lurked in her blue eyes and the tiny tucks at the corners of her mouth, Dave wondered how long it would be before he'd be free to hold her in his arms and love her as thoroughly as she deserved to be loved.

"At any rate, day after day, I would question him, and day after day, he would give me the same answer. So, you see, I had to pay attention. He was getting quite annoyed with me."

"Um-hmm," he agreed absently.

"One day, in exasperation, he suggested that I visit you and see for myself. I agreed, and that was when I called you. Then I had to wait so I would make connections with Jennifer."

Jennifer snapped to attention, forcing herself to ignore the waves of heat that Dave's sensual approval had unleashed. "Me?" she asked in astonishment. "You didn't even know me."

"That made it a bit more difficult," Tillie agreed absently. "But as soon as you sat next to me in the airplane, I knew—" Skidding to a stop, she put two fingers to her lips and cleared her throat.

Jennifer eyed her uneasily. "Knew what?"

"I'm in line first," Dave interrupted smoothly, glaring at his aunt. She was a notorious matchmaker and the last thing he wanted was to have her drop a heavy-handed hint to a lady who was already checking out her running shoes.

Tillie nodded with obvious relief. "That's right. But once we met, I thought that Jennifer should know, and then when I got here, just to be safe, I told everyone else."

Dave narrowed his eyes. The pieces were slowly falling into place and he didn't like the picture that was forming. "Aunt Tillie," he ordered, "in plain, simple and direct words, tell me what Uncle Walter said."

Jennifer ignored the plaintive gaze aimed at her and added her support. "Tell him, Aunt Tillie."

Tillie reached out and patted Dave's hand. "I'm sure he didn't mean it. You know how he loves riddles."

"Aunt Tillie, spill it!"

Folding her hands in her lap, she took a shaky breath and said, "Walter said that you would be having trouble with your heart this summer. Bad trouble," she added, her eyes dim with pain.

Dave stared at her, speechless. He had thought she was leading up to something bizarre, and he was right. She had outdone any of her previous efforts this time. In terms of all-out weirdness, this episode took the proverbial cake. Then a cold trickle moved down his spine when he thought of Walter's track record.

"I don't believe it," he said flatly. "I'm as healthy as a horse. My last physical said so."

"When was it?" Jennifer asked.

"It was just . . . not long ago," he hedged.

"Try putting that in months."

He grimaced. "Thirty-six."

"It's been three *years* since you've had a checkup? Anything could have happened in that time!"

"Do I look like I'm sick?" he demanded.

"Don't be cute, Dave. That has nothing to do with it, and you know it."

"All right, let's try this. I know how I feel and that's fine. My weight is normal, I don't smoke—"

"You eat foods with too much cholesterol."

"I get plenty of exercise—"

"And you should see a doctor."

He raked his hand through his hair. "Right. And what do I tell him? That my—" he stopped and glanced at Aunt Tillie "—deceased uncle sent a message that I should get my heart checked?"

"For heaven's sake! Just go in and get a physical."

"Of course," Tillie said in a consoling voice, "there's always a chance that Walter could be mistaken this time. Not a big one," she said honestly, "but a chance is better than nothing. Besides, Maybelle thinks you're fine."

Dave turned back to her. "Maybelle who?"

Tillie waved toward the open door. "You know— Maybelle."

A spasm crossed his face and his gaze switched from one woman to the other. "Do I want to hear this?" One look at Tillie's face convinced him. "No, by God, I don't. At least promise me this much: you're *not* going to tell me that you've been talking to the llamas!"

Tillie stood up and shook out her dress. She patted Dave on the shoulder and moved toward the door. "Of course not," she soothed. "I wouldn't dream of it."

Realizing that he had been holding his breath, he let it out with a hiss, relaxing as the tight nerves in his nape slowly unwound.

When she was safely outside, Tillie turned and ducked her head back in the room. "I'm going to let Jennifer tell you all about it."

Chapter Eight

Jennifer's grin turned into outright laughter when Dave turned to her. Despite the fact that she had been left to explain Tillie's absurd news, the sight of his frustrated glare was balm to her soul. Justice did prevail, after all. Or, to quote the modern day oracles, "What goes around, comes around." Dave, who had kept her in a state of muddled anxiety since the day she'd arrived, was getting a healthy dose of his own.

"Well?" he demanded, getting up and towering over her.

Her eyes were still bright with humor when she looked at him and shrugged. "What do you want me to say? She talks to llamas."

Swearing softly, he reached for her hand and tugged her to her feet, letting her own momentum carry her against him. Before she could protest, he wrapped his arms around her and held her close.

For a moment, the roar of blood racing through her body closed out every other sensation. When it subsided, she felt the thudding of his heart matching the rhythm of her own, felt his warm, hard-muscled body taking her weight, smelled the essence of sunshine and leather and man. She wound her arms around his neck, sighing when his hands separated and tightened, one between her shoulders, the other sliding down to the small of her back.

He hugged her, then with a sharp sigh, slid his hands into the back pockets of her jeans, keeping her pressed against his hips. "Okay, what's this all about?"

Jennifer leaned back, bracing her hands on his shoulders. She had a question of her own. "What do you suppose she meant about making connections with me?" she asked, watching his face like a hawk. "Surely Aunt Tillie couldn't have known about me in advance. Could she?" She felt the tension in her body dissipating when he shook his head and shrugged.

It was an effort, but Dave kept his face expressionless. "Damned if I know." And damned if he would say one thing that would make her more leery than she already was. It didn't take a genius to figure out that Richard, aside from being a royal pain in the butt, had been pretty heavy-handed. Jennifer didn't need Aunt Tillie arranging her life now. "What about the llamas?"

He felt the jolt when she smiled and wondered for a split second if there *was* something wrong with his heart.

"It's the craziest thing I've ever heard," she told him, grinning, "but I honestly think I believe her."

"Does she actually talk to them?"

Lifting one hand from his shoulder, she tapped her temple with a slim finger. "Telepathy."

He groaned and she collapsed against him, her laughter rippling around him, binding him to her with radiant ties of joy. "I don't believe it," he finally said.

"Why would she lie?" Jennifer asked, rubbing her cheek against his shirt.

He shook his head. "She may evade the issue, but I've never known her to lie."

"Well, I believe that *she* believes she's talking to them." She felt the warmth of his hands in her pockets, shaping her bottom, and tried to move away. Dave merely flexed his fingers and tugged her closer. "Let's put it this way, if she didn't do some heavy research about llamas before she came, she *is* talking to them."

"Why do you say that?" He nuzzled her earlobe, touching it with the tip of his tongue, and forgot the question almost as soon as he asked it. He had noticed that first afternoon in the truck that Jennifer didn't wear perfume. It didn't matter. Her fragrance was an intoxicating blend of freshness and sweet, warm woman. He would know it anywhere. Anytime.

"I think that we should sit down and talk," she said in a breathless voice that tried and failed to sound practical. "Not this way!" she yelped when he dropped down on the couch with her in his lap. Taking a deep breath, she said, "You here," stabbing a finger in his shoulder to keep him where he was, "and me there." She pointed to the opposite end of the couch.

His hold on her loosened. Slowly. And his hands managed to brush her thighs, her hips and the sides of her breasts before he released her. Her face was pink by the time she settled in the other corner, and the hands she raised to push back her hair were shaking.

Jennifer brushed busily at her jeans, avoiding his persistent gaze. When she raised her head, she looked no higher than his cheekbones. "Now," she said briskly, "where were we?"

"Llamas," he said lazily.

"Oh. Yeah. Aunt Tillie told me her news the day Amaryllis had her baby."

He straightened, his gaze no longer amused. "Why did it take you so long to tell me?"

"In the first place," she said, refusing to be intimidated, "it wasn't my secret. Aside from that, I can just imagine your reaction if I *had* told you. You probably would have locked me up and thrown away the key!"

"Thanks, Doc. No, I wasn't really worried. Just wanted to start out with a clean slate. Yeah, I'll give her your regards. Right. You'll be invited." Dave cradled the receiver and looked out the window of his office. A clean slate. All the test results were in, and that's what he had.

In the five days since Aunt Tillie had dropped her bomb, he had been in and out of more doctors' offices than he could count. He hadn't intended to go, but between Jen's arguments and the thought that Uncle Walter could just possibly be right, he had thrown in the towel. The one last barrier had been in not knowing what to tell Dr. Carter.

Doc had tended him most of his life and knew that he didn't call for an appointment until he had exhausted all his other options. He never voluntarily went in for a physical. The one he'd had three years ago had been done over his loud and profane objections. Doc had refused to saw a cast off his leg until he'd submitted to all the tests.

A smile curved his lips when he thought of how he had explained all of that to Jen—adding that he couldn't very well tell Doc the truth. She'd rounded on him like a spitting cat.

"You're inventive," she said. "Make something up. Tell him anything. Just go!"

His smile broadened to a grin when he thought of what her reaction would be to the story he'd concocted. He'd have to tell her soon, before she ran into Doc somewhere, because the old man would be sure to ask if she was the gorgeous flatlander who wouldn't marry Dave McGraw until he had a clean bill of health.

His grin faded, the thought reminding him of her first marriage. It wasn't a subject he liked to dwell on. After his first look at Jennifer at the airport, he'd known that she was his woman, and had wondered how long it would take her to reach the same conclusion. Learning that she'd lived with another man for four years had given him a few sleepless nights.

He'd known right away that she had undoubtedly given the marriage her best shot. When it hadn't worked, she'd ended it. More than likely, she'd waited far too long. Legally, it was over—but there were always more than legal aspects to a marriage. Emotional links were harder to sever.

According to Jen, Richard—the cretin—was a good man. That could be, but he was also a blind one. And one who got no sympathy from Dave McGraw, because in his blindness, Richard had done the unforgivable. He had deliberately set about diminishing Jen, and, to a degree, he'd succeeded. But not permanently, thank God. The fool had had no idea of what he'd held between his hands.

Dave scowled as he gazed out at the distant hills. Jennifer didn't talk much about the years she'd spent with him. She didn't have to. Seeing how she'd changed since she'd been at the ranch told him enough. In less than a month, her laugh had become free and spontaneous, her rich, tawny hair unrestrained. Her walk, in those snug jeans, told the world that she knew she was a woman with all her parts in the right place. A far cry from the lovely but muted woman at the airport who'd worn prim, ladylike clothes and had her hair tied in a cool knot at the back of her neck.

If he had to guess, he'd say that Richard had systematically stripped Jen of her spontaneity, her warmth, her feelings of self-worth, and finally, her love of life. Now it was up to Dave to make sure that she got it all back. No, he amended silently, moving over to the window and unconsciously evaluating the density of the moving gray clouds, not all of it. She had done most of that herself. The only remaining evidence of her ex-husband's handiwork was in her occasional moments of self-doubt.

Right now, she was working hard to prove something to herself. Too hard. She was in the midst of a double session of training classes. The party had netted her so many volunteers that she'd had to divide them up between day and evening sessions. So, he thought grimly, she was busy, and he was keeping his distance. As much as he could.

He had learned something the night of the party. He had enjoyed setting it up and handing her a roomful of volunteers, he had anticipated her look of pleasure when she saw the classroom. Of course, he admitted, it hadn't been done without an ulterior motive. He'd figured that the closer he kept her to the ranch, the sooner she'd learn to love it. And she *had* to love it if he was going to convince her to forget about California and make Montana her home. But afterward, he'd realized two things. Even though she was delighted with the classes, his actions had probably been as manipulative as her ex-husband's. And although her face had reflected genuine surprise and happiness, her sense of fulfillment would have been greater if she'd had a hand in organizing it.

So, as much as he wanted to anticipate her needs and hand everything to her on a silver platter, he wouldn't. Since his assistance seemed to detract from her sense of satisfaction, he'd back off and give her room—at least until she realized that other people needed to give as much as she did. When she remembered that, he had the feeling that she would be healed. From that point on, they'd slug it out toe-to-

toe, each giving and taking. He grinned in pure anticipation at the thought. He just hoped it didn't take too
long. This had been strictly a cerebral decision; his
body was fighting it every step of the way.

After punching a few buttons on the intercom, he
waited, then said to Irma, "I'm going over to Len's
place to see his new tractor. Be back in several hours."

"Hi, Aunt Tillie." Jennifer dropped down on the
bench overlooking the broad meadow. Some distance
away, the llamas grazed peacefully. Browsed, she corrected herself. Maybelle had been quite explicit about
that. While grazers confined themselves to grass,
browers supplemented the grass with twigs and leaves
from bushes and young trees.

"I see that they're right on time," she said, nodding at the llamas. The animals followed a strict rou-
tine. Early in the morning they were in the sunniest
spot available. By midmorning they were working
their way across the meadow, and their afternoons
were spent down by the stream. Evenings, they stayed
close to the buildings, hoping to mooch some grain or
alfalfa hay.

"You look thoughtful," Jennifer commented,
marveling at her own ability for understatement. The
tiny, preoccupied woman looked as if she had been
asked to come up with the solution for world peace—
in one week.

Tillie blinked. "What, dear?"

"Are you all right, Aunt Tillie?" Jennifer's gaze
deepened with concern.

"I'm fine," Tillie said absently, staring out at the llamas with a slight frown. "Well, actually, a little puzzled."

"Oh."

"And confused."

"Umm."

"Frustrated, too, I suppose."

"Ah."

"And concerned."

"I'm sorry, is there anything I can do?"

Tugging thoughtfully at a silver curl, Tillie said, "Not right now, dear. Maybe later."

Jennifer watched the older woman's gaze slide to the right and focus on the lone animal at the far end of the green stretch. Paladin. "Is he the problem?" she asked gently.

Tillie's sigh was a blend of exasperation and distress. "I don't know why I let him bother me."

As if responding to an unheard signal, Paladin lifted his head and stared straight at her. The others moved slowly toward the trees bordering the creek. Jennifer knew that once they crossed the wooden plank bridge they would almost be out of sight. There the ground sloped at a steeper angle and the trees grew thicker, all but concealing a rutted road that the men occasionally used. Dave had once taken her on a maintenance run all the way to the end, where he checked food supplies that had been left in a small shack. Emergency provisions for backpackers, he'd explained.

"Are you sure I can't do something, Aunt Tillie? You know that you have only to ask."

Tillie reached out and patted her hand. "Such a sweet girl," she murmured. "I knew that you'd be perfect for—" She blinked and slid a guilty look at Jennifer. "It's just that I've had a little shock," she explained. "It brought back some memories and I just need time to sort things out."

Alarmed, Jennifer held on to the small hand. "Do you want me to get Dave? Would you like to talk to him?"

Shaking her head, Tillie said, "I'll be fine. Besides, I saw him leave in the truck a few minutes ago."

As the two women sat, each buried in her own thoughts, Paladin moved in the general direction the others had taken. Traveling at that angle, Jennifer estimated, he would arrive at the stream a little above them, but within sight.

"I followed him yesterday," Tillie said abruptly.

Jennifer tilted her head in Paladin's direction and raised her brows inquiringly.

Tillie nodded. "I took a leaf out of Mac's book and hid behind the trees until I got close. When I did, I made a noise and he turned around and looked right at me."

Jennifer waited until it was obvious that Tillie was through. "What happened then?" The look she got was complex and far from comforting. Jennifer stiffened and drew in a deep breath, preparing for the worst.

"It wasn't anything he did," Tillie muttered. "He... No, you won't believe it. *I'm* still having a hard time accepting it. And if I can't, how can I expect you—"

"For heaven's sake, Aunt Tillie, *what*?"

Tillie blinked and took a quick breath. "He has Walter's eyes," she said in a rush.

Staring at the petite woman, Jennifer opened her mouth, then closed it without saying a word. *I don't believe it,* she thought.

"I knew you wouldn't," Tillie said calmly.

"Oh, Aunt Tillie, I wouldn't hurt you for the world, but do you know how preposterous it sounds? Do you realize what you're implying?"

"Even more than you do, Jennifer."

"But, how can you possibly..."

"I believe that we all return in some form or another. Walter did, too. And he *has* been gone for twelve years. It's not impossible. I don't think this is my first time around, do you?"

"Do I what?"

"Think it's your first time?"

Jennifer stared at her, intrigued in spite of herself. "I don't know. I've never thought about it."

"Walter gave it a great deal of thought. He used to joke and say that if he was good enough in *this* life, perhaps he'd get his harem in the next. And then, of course, there's the name."

"Name?" Jennifer repeated numbly. "Whose?"

"His." She waved toward the llama. "Theirs. Paladin means powerful warrior or champion."

"From the first, you were calling him Warrior," Jennifer said, recalling the conversation at the table the night they'd arrived.

Tillie nodded. "Yes. That's what I picked up every time he was mentioned. It was my pet name for Walter," she added softly.

"But what does that have to do with—"

"Walter," she said softly, "also means powerful warrior."

"Oh, God."

"But you're not to worry," Tillie said briskly. "Paladin may be the strong, silent type, but I'm still in touch with Walter every day."

"What does *he* say about it?"

"Well, to be honest, he's being most annoying. He's in one of his enigmatic phases, and he isn't answering my questions. Aside from that, he's very full of himself these days, which, added to the other . . . unusual circumstances, merely strengthens my suspicions." Smiling at Jennifer, she said, "Have you been getting too much sun, dear? You look a little peculiar."

Jennifer shook her head. "No, I feel fine," she said unconvincingly. "Really."

"How far are you into your training classes?" Tillie asked.

"Halfway," Jennifer said, blinking at the sudden change of subject. Evidently, when Tillie was through discussing something, she was through. She didn't even *try* to be subtle. "I divided the required twelve hours into four three-hour classes. We have the weekend off, then we'll finish next week."

"I suppose you have something that you have to do now," Tillie said.

"Yes," Jennifer said with a wry smile, leaning down to kiss the other woman's soft cheek, "actually, I do. If you need me, I'll be in my cabin." Looking up at the overcast sky, she said, "It looks like it might rain in a while. You'll be sure to get inside in plenty of time, won't you?"

Tillie nodded. "I'll watch," she promised. "But I never catch cold."

Jennifer eyed the sky again as she walked back to the cabin. The dark clouds were moving fast and the tips of the pine trees undulated in the sudden breeze. In California the weather always managed to surprise the residents. A gray and sullen sky could leave some areas bone-dry; in others, it could mean cloudbursts and mud slides. She had no idea what it meant in Montana.

She hadn't lied to Aunt Tillie, Jennifer thought several hours later, getting up from the desk to switch on the lights. She did have things to do—reports to make, lesson plans to review. She even had a textbook to study for the last class she needed to renew her credential. She had more than enough to keep her busy. It was unfortunate that she couldn't settle down to do any of it.

She could save both time and effort, Jennifer reflected, if she would just face up to her problem. And of course the big problem—at least six feet four inches of it—was Dave McGraw. In the last few days he had backed off a little, but he made no secret of the fact that he was waiting. And that was what was driving her crazy. What was he waiting for? What did he expect of her? She didn't have any more to give, and even if she had, she didn't know if she would.

Dave, on the other hand, was a man who enjoyed giving, which presented certain difficulties for a woman who also had trouble taking. What, she wondered, does a woman who insists on making her own way do with a man who gives her whatever she wants before she even knows she wants it? A complicated question, she thought dryly. Maybe she needed an Uncle Walter in her life to bounce the hard ones off on. Her only answer was, if the woman wants to be free, and she's smart, she runs!

And that was exactly what she was planning to do—as soon as the tutor-training classes were over and she showed a few people how to establish a literacy council. She couldn't possibly leave new tutors without a central support system, a place where they could get information, material and encouragement. Dave or no Dave, she had to remain that long.

Before she could give herself a pep talk and move back to the typewriter, a shrill warbling sound erupted outside her cabin. She spun around just in time to watch what looked like the entire herd of llamas pound past her door. The stampede ended in the meadow, she noted, craning her neck out of the window. The llamas gathered around Tillie, who was still seated on the bench and, judging by their agitated shuffling, were telling her what had incited them to panic.

Shaking her head, she headed back to the desk, grinning as she thought of Dave's reaction to the latest llama episode. She was mentally rehearsing the story when Tillie, holding her skirt up so she could run, dashed into the cabin.

"Walter's in trouble!" she panted.

Jennifer spun around, taking in Tillie's pink cheeks and distracted air. *"Walter?"* Blinking at the small woman, she wondered how on earth one helped someone in the spirit world.

Tillie threw up her hands, dropping her skirt. "Paladin, Walter, whatever, he's in trouble and I'm going to help him!" she declared, backing away.

"Wait a minute!" Jennifer bolted across the room to block the door. "I'm not trying to stop you," she said, lying through her teeth. She'd wrestle Aunt Tillie to the floor and sit on her before she'd let her out that door. "But, if he needs help, he probably needs more than we can give him. Let's get some of the men."

Before she got there, Tillie moved back to stand in the open doorway. "No, you know what a loner he is. He won't let any of the men close to him. He needs me, and I'm going. I just stopped to tell you so someone would know."

Jennifer cast a distracted glance at the threatening sky. "Aunt Tillie, you *can't* go. You can't walk around on rough ground in those clothes. You need a jacket and boots. And it's going to rain. You'll get pneumonia."

Tillie took a quick glance of her own at the dark clouds. "You can loan me a jacket," she said calmly, remaining in the doorway. She hitched up her skirt to show Jennifer her orange high-top tennis shoes. "These will do just fine, and I never get sick. Don't try to stop me," she said, watching Jennifer's face. "I'm going, with or without a jacket."

"All right," Jennifer got out through clenched teeth. "But you're not going without me, and you're going to give me five minutes to grab some things. You can sit down and tune in to Walter while you're waiting!"

She pulled Tillie inside and slammed the cabin door. Running into the bedroom, she threw open the closet and grabbed a small, lightweight backpack. "I must be crazy," she muttered, tossing a nylon poncho, a couple of sweaters and a jacket on the bed. "Taking off in what looks like it's going to be the granddaddy of all storms, chasing after a llama who can probably take better care of himself than we can. A llama who may or may not be a man who's been dead for a dozen years."

Jennifer added a flashlight and a box of matches to the pile on the bed. Grabbing several pairs of socks out of the drawer, she kept one pair and dropped the others on the growing pile. She kicked off her sandals, then put on the socks and running shoes. "Dave is going to kill me," she told herself grimly. "Letting an old lady go out in this weather. I should have my head examined."

"Age is a state of mind," Tillie called from the other room. "I'm not old. Are you almost ready?"

Jennifer scooped up the stuff from the bed and carried it out to the couch. "Put on these sweaters," she ordered briskly, "and the poncho. I think the sky is going to split wide open any minute."

"What are you going to wear?" Tillie asked, obediently stuffing her arms into the sweaters and rolling up the cuffs.

"The jacket is water-repellent." Jennifer's voice was muffled as she pulled a sweatshirt over her head. She yanked it down to her hips and ran into the kitchen. After a quick survey, she swept up a box of breakfast bars and several oranges. "This will have to do. Here, wear this." She tossed Tillie a yellow sun hat with a wide brim. "It'll keep the water out of your eyes." She pulled her own hair back and tied it at her nape with a scarf.

Stuffing everything but the flashlight into the knapsack, she turned to survey the older woman. It was a good thing that Tillie wasn't overly concerned about the clothes she wore, Jennifer thought. Because, at the moment, she looked like a plump little teapot with a bright yellow lid. The beige poncho floated around her, held out at an angle by the bulk of two sweaters and Tillie's swirling skirts.

Jennifer shrugged into her jacket and worked her arms through the straps of the knapsack. "Less than five minutes," she said, taking a quick peek at her watch. "Ready?"

Tillie nodded and stepped out the door. Jennifer followed, her eyes darting to Dave's place, hoping to see his truck. "He's not back yet," she muttered in disgust, buttoning her jacket against the rising wind. "The man's around all hours of the day, except when you need him."

"Just like a man," Tillie agreed, spreading her arms to hold down the sides of the poncho.

"Wait a minute." Jennifer knelt beside her. "Let me button the sides of this thing, otherwise it's going to have you levitating. There." She looked around. "Which way?"

"Maybelle said to cross the plank bridge and turn right on the trail."

"Did she tell you what happened? Oh, wait a minute, there's Mac in the barn." He came to the open doorway and cocked his head when she yelled, his rapt stare concentrated on Tillie. "Mac," Jennifer called, "Paladin's in trouble and we're going after him." Without removing his eyes from Tillie, he nodded.

Jennifer stayed close to Tillie as they worked their way down to the bridge. "The water seems higher than it usually is," she said in concern as fat drops of rain bounced on the ground all around them. "It must be raining somewhere else and draining into the stream. If it gets too high, we might not be able to get back." She looked into Tillie's eyes. "Are you sure we should do this? Can't we wait?"

Tillie shook her head. "Rustlers were after Walter," she said definitely. "He got away, but we should be there in case they try again."

"Rustlers? We're going after *rustlers*? Barehanded? Aunt Tillie, this is crazy!" But she followed the determined woman across the bridge.

Tillie's voice was tranquil. "Stupid rustlers who work in the daytime shouldn't be any problem. Especially if they can't hold on to what they rustle." She touched Jennifer's arm. "We won't have any trouble, I promise you."

"How did Walt—Paladin get away?" Jennifer asked, leading Tillie toward the safest footing.

"When one man got close, he spit in his face."

"I still don't understand," Jennifer asked, "why everyone talks about llama spit as if it's worse than a curse."

"Well," Tillie said objectively, "when you consider that it's partly regurgitated food—"

Jennifer swallowed convulsively. "I'm sorry I asked."

Chapter Nine

Dave eased the truck to a stop at the side of his house and ran for the back door, taking the steps three at a time. He stepped into the service porch and peeled off his wet things. Padding through to his bedroom, he pulled on dry pants and finished buttoning his shirt by the living room window.

Jennifer's light was on. It gleamed a welcome and it was all he could do to keep from wandering over to see what she was doing. It had been too long since he had seen her blue eyes smile at him. No, he told himself, a grim set to his mouth, he was giving her time and space. He'd meet her in the lodge for dinner. In just about three hours, he thought after a quick glance at his watch. No big deal. He had plenty of odds and ends to catch up on. He'd manage to keep busy. Pass the time. Somehow.

An hour later, he looked up from the computer, swearing softly. He had done about five minutes of work since he'd started and he was tired of watching a blinking cursor. Tapping a key, he exited the program and watched the light fade from the screen.

Five minutes later he was at the lodge, following Irma around the kitchen. "I'm back," he announced unnecessarily, snagging a couple of chocolate chip cookies from a plate.

"Did you come over to tell me that or to eat all the cookies?" she asked dryly, swatting at his hand as he reached for more.

He grabbed another one before she swung the plate out of reach. "No, I thought I'd go in and visit with Aunt Tillie for a while."

"Such a loving nephew," Irma said, dumping a couple of cookie sheets in the sink to soak. "This visit wouldn't have anything to do with the fact that you're hoping Jenny will get lonely and come looking for you over here, would it?"

"You're a nosy woman," he retorted, picking up an orange. "Besides, she's more likely to come here than to my place."

"Whatever your intentions, you're out of luck. Unless maybe Tillie is in her room. I haven't see her since lunch."

Surprise flickered in his eyes. "That's odd. With the weather the way it is, I thought she'd be tucked in the TV room watching some sci-fi horror flick."

"Nope." Irma slapped a hunk of beef on the cutting board. "Last time I saw her she was sitting on the old park bench in the meadow."

"Maybe she's down at the barn talking to Mac," he said with a grin.

Irma pulled out a paper bag, poured some flour into it, dropped in chunks of meat and shook the sack. "You talk about a combination," she said with a chuckle, "those two take the cake. She can't figure out why he's so fascinated with her, and he thinks she's been kicked out of Las Vegas."

Dave swallowed his last cookie and stood up. "Yeah, at one time he thought she was a rustler."

"Tillie?" Irma looked up from dropping the dredged meat in sizzling oil. "A rustler?"

"Yeah." He grinned again. "Had a hell of a time convincing him that she was my aunt." Dave shrugged into his slicker and opened a cupboard door, pulling a smaller raincoat out. "I'll take this one with me in case she's stuck down there without a jacket."

Thinking that she might be indulging in her latest fad, he stopped at the bunkhouse first to see if she had conned any of the men into a card game. When he found the place dark, he went on to the barn.

"Mac?" he called, opening the door.

"Yeah?" Mac looked up. He was sitting on a small three-legged stool, in the midst of a conversation with Nick and John.

Nodding to the men, Dave said, "I came down to collect Aunt Tillie."

"From where?" Mac asked. "She ain't here."

"Are you sure?"

Mac gave him a patient look. "Sure I'm sure. We're sittin' here talkin', ain't we? If she was here, she'd be whipping a deck of cards out of one of her crazy skirts and stealing all the matchsticks in the place." The other two men grinned at what was obviously a much-discussed grievance. "I ain't seen her since late this afternoon. About a couple of hours ago, I guess."

Dave narrowed his eyes in thought, the first flicker of alarm nudging him. He didn't claim to have any of Tillie's psychic sensitivity. He didn't need any. He knew his aunt and her talent for finding trouble. He wasn't really worried, he told himself, shrugging away the sudden tension in his shoulders. He'd just feel a hell of a lot better when he found her.

"She's probably down at Jennifer's," he said, turning and heading out the door, unbuttoning the slicker.

The rain had stopped, but it would be back. He cast an experienced eye at the dark sky that shrouded the mountaintops. When it came, it wouldn't have the power of what was happening up there, but they'd still feel the effects of it down here. As he walked, Dave pictured the water running off the saturated ground, sheeting off slabs of rock, forming streams that linked with others, repeating the process until it was a seething wall thundering down the mountain, pouring into rivers and filling creeks until they overflowed their banks.

"Jennifer?" Dave nudged the door open with a light, triple knock. "Jen?" When he got no answer, he stepped in. Lights were blazing, the typewriter was humming, but the cabin was empty. The flicker of alarm that he'd felt before was developing into an incandescent flare. He felt it all the way to his bones. Something was wrong.

He strode into the bedroom and took a quick, comprehensive look around. One of Jennifer's sandals lay close to the bathroom, the other in the doorway of the closet. When he bent over to pick that one up, his gaze swept the clothing hanging on the rod. A second glance didn't tell him much more than the first had. On the third try, his hand tightened suddenly on the small, flexible shoe. He had wasted precious seconds wondering what he expected to find in her closet. It was what *wasn't* there that gave him the clue he was looking for, he realized. Among all the blouses, skirts, dresses, prim pleated slacks and folded jeans, there was not one warm sweater. Not a jacket, not a sweatshirt. Nothing. And at one time or another he had seen her wear a bunch of them.

It took him less than a minute to search the entire cabin. Nothing. No warm clothes at all. Not bothering with the lights, he slammed the door and ran back to the barn.

"Mac?" He burst through the door, startling the three men. "Just where was it that you saw Aunt Tillie?"

"Heading down toward the creek. She was with Miss Jenny."

Dave felt his heart jolt as a series of disjointed images ran through his mind, all of them centering on the two women being swept away by a wall of water. "What were they wearing?"

Mac snorted. "I don't know nuthin' about women's clothes, especially the kind Miss Tillie wears." A reluctant grin curved his lips. "She looked like a little haystack." His amusement faded and he aimed a severe glance at Dave. "If I was you and that old lady was *my* aunt, I'd be ashamed to let her go around dressed in curtains. 'Course," he mused, "if she played poker for cash instead of matches, she could afford to buy some decent clothes."

Someday, Dave decided, he would tell Mac about the value of Southern California property and describe Aunt Tillie's Spanish-style home in the exclusive area of Rancho Santa Fe. And, if he was feeling up to it, he might even explain how Walter, acting as her financial advisor, had helped her to quadruple the healthy nest egg he had left for her when he'd died. But not now.

"Haystack?" He scowled at the old man.

Shrugging, Mac tried again. "She had on a light brown thing that just kind of hung over all that other stuff she had on. And a big yellow hat that tied under the chin."

Dave shook his head. The vagaries of Tillie's wardrobe were beyond him. "What about Jen? What did she have on?"

Mac brightened. "Jeans and a jacket. And one of them little backpacks," he added helpfully.

Dave's face paled. "Nick," he snapped, "get on the intercom and tell Irma to check every room in the lodge for Aunt Tillie and Jen. Stay on the line until she gets back to you. John, you get some of the others and check the classroom, the tack room and every one of the outbuildings. Now!" The two younger men exchanged a wordless glance and disappeared.

"Mac, did anything happen today while I was gone? Anything unusual?"

The old man screwed up his face in thought and squinted through the door that John had left open. "Like what?" he asked finally.

"Hell, I don't know. Anything!"

"You mean like the llamas?"

Closing his eyes, Dave took a deep breath and said, "Let's start there."

"Well, late this afternoon—"

"Before you saw Tillie and Jen?"

"Yeah. I heard this noise that sounded like a turkey had sat on a hot wire."

The alarm that the llamas gave when they were threatened. Dave tensed. "Go on."

"They all came stampeding up from the creek and hustled down to the meadow. Come to think of it, they gathered around Miss Tillie and they were all humming something fierce. Pretty soon, she got up and hightailed it to Miss Jenny's place."

Dave hardly breathed. "Then what?"

Mac shrugged. "I stepped back in here for a minute. When I went back out, they was heading for the creek. Miss Jenny spotted me and waved. She called out something about Paladin and they went on walkin'."

"Did Paladin come back with the others?"

"Hell, I don't know. I didn't take a nose count. They pounded past here like the devil himself was on their tail." He looked at Dave's drawn face. "What are you so riled up about?"

"I'm beginning to think," Dave said roughly, "that they're on the other side of the bridge." He moved over to a small storage room. "Give me a hand with this stuff," he ordered. "If Nick and John don't find them, I want to be ready."

Mac automatically helped him with the emergency rescue equipment. "They wouldn't do that," he protested. "The backpack's ready to go," he said, interrupting himself when Dave hefted it. "Everything on the checklist is in it. They wouldn't do it," he repeated. "Even a kid would know better than that!"

"A kid who was born out here would," Dave agreed grimly. "But they're from a city. They're used to drains in the streets and flood control systems. They probably wouldn't even think of high water or flash floods."

Nick and John arrived almost at the same time. "Irma says they're not there."

"No sign of them, Dave, and the bridge is already under water."

The four men stared at each other with grim eyes.

Dave moved to the door, tossing orders over his shoulder. "John, run down to the cabin and get a warm change of clothes for Jennifer. Mac, call Irma and tell her to do the same for Aunt Tillie. Nick, get the clothes in the pack and toss it in the back of my rig. Throw in a couple of extra sleeping bags and tie a tarp over the truck bed. I'll take it from there."

"I'll go with you," Nick offered.

Dave shook his head. "I'll find them. I want the rest of you to keep an eye on things around here. Don't let any of the guests wander close to the water."

"Be careful, Aunt Tillie," Jennifer panted, trying to keep one eye on the slippery trail winding relentlessly upward and the other one on the cheerful woman walking contentedly beside her. The rain had slowed down to a steady drizzle. "Exactly what did Maybelle and the others tell you?"

"She said that they were all taken by surprise. They were munching on some new shoots by the stream when two men appeared from the direction of the road. They tried to maneuver Walter—"

"Paladin."

"—into their truck. He really acted quite heroically," she said proudly. "He sounded the alarm, told the others to get back to the meadow, and that he would take care of himself. That sounds just like Walter," she beamed. "Maybelle saw him spit at one man and bite the other. Then he took off on this trail."

"It sounds to me like he had everything under control. My next question is, what are we doing here?" She brushed a dripping branch out of her way and added, "No, let me rephrase that. I know why *I'm* here—because I couldn't let you come by yourself. What I don't understand is why you were so determined to do it."

Tillie sighed. "Because I have to be here. Why, I'm not really sure, but the strength of the—" she waved a hand, searching for the right word "—vibrations is overwhelming. I admit that when I ran to your cabin, I was as distraught as Maybelle and the others, thinking that Walter was in dreadful danger, but while I waited for you, I had time to recover. And think."

"About what?"

Reaching up to adjust her hat, Tillie said, "I'll be going home soon. Now that I know David is all right, I can—"

Jennifer stopped, as much to catch her breath as to examine the expression on the older woman's face. "Wait a minute. He hasn't heard about his test results. How can you know?"

Tillie's shrug was a masterpiece of delicacy. "The same way I knew there would be a problem."

Resuming the uphill trek, Jennifer said wryly, "Somehow—since you say there *is* no problem—that answer doesn't exactly inspire me with confidence."

"No, there is definitely something, but apparently it won't affect his health. It will all be quite clear. Soon. Of course," Tillie complained mildly, "none of this would have happened if Walter hadn't acted like a mystic oracle speaking in riddles. And the annoying part is that he'll say the misunderstanding is all my fault."

They walked in silence until they reached a fork in the trail. Tillie unhesitatingly pointed to the right.

"I have the strongest feeling that Walter has found himself a snug little retreat," she announced.

"Walter the man or the llama?"

Tillie's brows wrinkled under the droopy hat brim. "It *does* get confusing, doesn't it?"

"Especially to those of us who don't have ESP," Jennifer admitted, grinning. "For my sake, do you think we could call the llama Paladin?"

Tillie nodded reluctantly. "As long as you understand—"

"I do," Jennifer said hurriedly. "Really. You were going to tell me why it was so important to come up here," she reminded her.

"Because I have to talk with Wa—Paladin. I thought that if the two of us could be alone together for a while, he'd *have* to talk to me. You see," she said earnestly, "I don't *mind* if he has a harem—as long as he's a llama. It's not knowing for sure that's so vexing. And that's another thing. Walter always promised me that if he came back, I would be the first to know. Now, I think he is back, and he won't say a word. But I have my suspicions about that. Do you know what I think?"

Jennifer shook her head, wide-eyed with fascination. "I haven't the foggiest."

"I think that he got caught up in a twist of fate. Destiny gone awry," Tillie said, her eyes bright with speculation.

"Karma?" ventured Jennifer, trying to hold up her end of the conversation.

Tillie beamed. "Exactly! Hoist with his own petard, as the English say. You see, Walter was, in his own quiet way, quite a practical joker. He would set up elaborate and quite outrageous plots, involve one of his poor, unsuspecting friends, then watch with glee as the poor soul tried to talk his way out of the situation."

Trying to follow Tillie's convoluted logic, Jennifer took several more steps before realizing that she was alone. When she stopped and looked back, Tillie was watching her, head tilted, waiting expectantly. Jennifer took a deep breath, then slowly released it. "Are you really saying what I think you are?'' Tillie's raised brows encouraged her. ''Are you telling me that Walter warned you about Dave, then, when you decided to come to see him, some mischievous force brought Walter back as Paladin, putting him in such an awkward position that he couldn't tell you about it?''

Tillie's smile was blinding. ''Isn't it delicious?''

The pickup, powered by its four-wheel drive, surged through the roiling water and snarled up the steep incline. Dave stuck his hand out of the open window and waved to the three men on the far side. Making a sharp right, he roared down the road that threaded back and forth across an old hiking trail.

The windshield wipers kept to a steady, monotonous pace, running in rhythm with thoughts that were as bleak as the sky above. Two women alone, probably soaked to the skin by now, night coming on, always the chance of a bear, no weapons, wouldn't know how to use them even if they had any. And that was only for starters. What the *hell* were they doing out here? They should be sitting in front of the fireplace in the lodge—or, in Jennifer's case, in his living room—looking warm and sweet and capable of loving a man to death.

Grim-faced, he stopped, vaulted out of the truck and made his way over to the trail. If there was anything good about the situation, he thought, eyes narrowed as he stepped carefully on the saturated ground, it was that the steady drizzle wasn't obliterating the tracks. And that two city women, slipping and sliding in mud, left signs so obvious that a blind man could follow them.

Loping back to the truck, he visualized the next point at which the road intersected the path. He would head for that one and if any marks were there, shoot on to the next. Repeating the pattern would be quicker than following them on foot. Once he reached a point where there were no more tracks, he'd take the pack and hike down to them. That way, he assured himself, he would reach them before the bears or hypothermia did.

"Aunt Tillie, are you all right?" Jennifer asked. Her worried glance flicked over her companion. Tillie's stamina was amazing, but the fact remained that she was almost three times Jennifer's age and needed to get dry and warm.

Tillie nodded cheerfully. "I told you, I never get sick. I'm not cold or wet enough to do myself any harm."

"I hate to complain, but can't you focus in on Paladin's warm, snug retreat a little better?" What she wanted to say was "faster." They had been on the trail for almost three hours and Tillie still insisted that it was a bit farther.

"It doesn't work like a zoom lens on a camera," Tillie explained patiently. "It's never that clear."

Jennifer groaned.

"But I'll know it when we get there."

"Are you sure?" Jennifer looked for signs of doubt on Tillie's face and found none.

"Positive."

"Well, I hope it's soon, because it's going to get dark before long. And even though we have a big flashlight, I'd just as soon not be stuck on this trail when it's pitch dark." And that had to be the understatement of the century, she decided, looking up at the rapidly fading light. Right now, she'd give just about everything she owned for the sight of a big, slightly overwhelming man who had a tendency to be managing and just a bit pushy. She was tired of being in charge. For the first time in a long time, she was willing—no, eager—to be taken care of.

But about all that she could hope for at this point was that Tillie shared her fears and would be spurred on to greater efforts. Unfortunately, Tillie's next words showed that not only did she not share them, she didn't even hear them.

"Just think, Jennifer." Tillie's voice seethed with excitement. "If I can get Paladin to talk to me, and he truly is Walter, I'll have an answer to the question that people have been asking almost from the beginning of time. I'll have positive proof that people do come back."

"I'll settle for finding out where we're going to spend the night," Jennifer answered, glancing worriedly around. The light was fading fast.

"I know this is difficult for you, but just have a little faith."

Easy for you to say, Jennifer thought. Faith in whom, or what? An enigmatic spirit who spoke in riddles and loved practical jokes? A llama?

"In me," Tillie said, gently chiding.

"I'm sorry, Aunt Tillie, but I'm worried. And I'm getting scared. We don't know for sure that Mac understood, so we can't count on Dave or any of the men coming to the rescue. And I don't know that much about—"

"There!" Tillie pointed to a black spot that loomed against the craggy terrain.

"Where?" Sheer terror lifted the hair on Jennifer's nape as her imagination provided her with visions of ten-foot bears and wolves with glistening fangs.

"That's it!"

At the note of satisfaction in Tillie's voice, Jennifer's heartbeat slowed down to merely frantic. "What?" she asked a little more calmly.

"That's where he is," Tillie whispered.

"Paladin?"

"Yes."

"Is he alone?" Jennifer asked faintly, suddenly remembering the original reason for their trek—the rustlers.

"The men never chased him," Tillie told her. "In fact, I have the feeling that they've just had a very unpleasant interview with Nick and some of the men. Let's go look. I believe that we're going to find a nice, snug cave."

Jennifer swallowed. "It isn't that I doubt you, Aunt Tillie, but let's not rush into this, okay? Paladin may be in there, but he might also have some company that we'd just as soon not meet." For the first time since they'd left the cabin, she turned on the flashlight. Together, they tiptoed silently toward the gaping black mouth.

The wide beam of light traveled in a circle around the outer rim of the cave. When nothing ghastly flew out, Jennifer grew bolder. Stepping closer, she swung the light in another quick circular survey, this time of the interior. The cave was small and didn't look very deep. Taking a quick breath, she lowered the beam and aimed right at the center.

A very alert-looking Paladin, banana ears erect, stared back at her. He was resting, legs folded beneath him, but appeared fully capable of leaping to his feet and bolting between them to escape.

"Walter! I knew we'd find you!" Tillie darted inside, bubbling with enthusiasm. "Finally. And just imagine, since we can't get back to the ranch tonight, we have hours and hours to talk!"

Paladin lifted his eyes heavenward and groaned.

"Hell!"

Dave threw himself back into the truck and sent it jolting up the road. Swearing steadily, he promised himself that when he found them, he would strangle them. Wiping perspiration from his cold forehead, he told himself that the clean bill of health Dr. Carter had given him was suspect, because his heart was bouncing between his stomach and his throat while beating at twice its usual rate.

He hadn't thought that they'd get so far. The last switchback had been the fifth, which meant they had traveled at least five miles. Considering the altitude, the weather and the steep incline, not to mention Tillie's age and the fact that neither of them had proper shoes, they were making good time. In fact, if he hadn't been so damned mad and worried, he'd be impressed.

What if one of them slipped? What if they both did? What if they were lying crumpled on the trail with broken bones, in shock? He made the next switchback in record time. The light was almost gone, but there was enough to see that there was nothing to see. Not a footstep, not a broken blade of grass or a turned stone. Muttering something that fell in the shady area between a curse and a prayer, he turned back to the truck and cut off the lights.

It shouldn't take long to work down to them, he decided, pulling on his backpack. Once he found them—after he strangled them—he'd get them warm and dry. Tomorrow, they could head down and see what shape the creek was in. Tonight was the problem, he reflected, his long legs making easy work of the narrow trail. Then again, maybe it wasn't. If his memory wasn't playing tricks on him, it was right in this area that he had spotted a cave. It wasn't big, but it might just fit the three of them. He could build a fire, have them change clothes and—

Rounding a sharp corner, Dave stopped and let his eyes feast on the most beautiful sight he had ever seen. A cave, just as he remembered it, eight or ten feet off the trail. It was illuminated by the most anemic little fire he'd ever seen. Tillie was seated on a rock while Jennifer—a bedraggled, dirty, absolutely breathtaking Jennifer—was standing over the fire rubbing her hands together. Paladin, the only one of the three who seemed to have any sense at all, was staring out into the dark straight at him.

As far as he could tell, Tillie was none the worse for wear. She was holding a limp yellow hat out to the fire and her silver curls were standing straight on end. Whatever else she was wearing had apparently kept her dry. His gaze switched to Jennifer and his eyes narrowed. Her jeans were dark from the rain, and even standing over the fire, she was shivering. He had been right about the size of the cave, he decided. It was hardly big enough for three; it definitely wouldn't hold four.

Moving closer, he heard Tillie's voice.

"I wonder what David is doing right now."

Stepping forward, he said pleasantly, "Deciding whether to strangle you now or save the pleasure for later."

Chapter Ten

David!"

"Dave!"

The two women cried out at the same time, Tillie in unqualified delight and Jennifer in shock. Paladin watched the proceedings with great interest.

Dave kept his voice matter-of-fact as he shrugged out of the backpack and knelt to fix the fire. "How did you get this started?"

"Luckily, someone had taken refuge here in the past," Tillie informed him brightly. "There's some wood stacked over there," she added, waving to a surprisingly large pile behind Paladin, "and Jennifer very cleverly got it going."

"I brought some matches," Jennifer said at the same time.

"Umm." His gaze slid up her wet jeans and jacket to her face. "Intending to stay awhile, were you?"

Grimacing at the restrained fury in his eyes, Jennifer clamped her teeth together and stepped back into the shadows behind him.

Damn it! Dave raged silently as he fed the fire, more furious than ever when he noticed the fine tremors in his hands. He had sworn that he would stay calm—after he'd strangled them—explain the dangers of rain and flash floods, and ask them politely just what in *hell* they thought they were doing. They had no right to risk their lives. Ever. Especially not now that he—

"David," Tillie exclaimed, "why are you so upset?"

"Upset?" he asked through clenched teeth. "What makes you think I'm upset? Your famous ESP?"

She blinked, considered him thoughtfully, then shook her head. "No. I think it's the bunched up muscles in your cheeks."

A choked sound came from behind him.

Dave rose to his full height, his shadow assuming awesome proportions in the small cave. "I am not upset," he stated evenly. "No, if we're going to be honest about this, I guess you could say that I'm so damn mad I could throttle you both. I drove over a bridge that I couldn't even see because it was under water, just to look for you. I've been driving like a madman on that muddy road wondering if I was going to find a couple of broken bodies. I've been—"

"David," Tillie interrupted tenderly, looking up at him with a depth of understanding that left him shaken. "Thank you, darling."

He stopped, took a deep breath and released it in a gusty sigh. He didn't want to be mollified, he decided. He wanted to put the fear of God in them, to yell a bit, swear a lot and get rid of the adrenaline pumping through his body. "For what?" he asked grudgingly.

"For loving us. For being frightened."

"Damn it, Aunt Tillie." He took the hand that she held out to him and brought her to her feet. Sweeping her up into a huge hug, he muttered into her silver curls, "The rest of us don't have your advantage. We have to be *told* things. Don't ever do this to me again." He squeezed her once more and set her on her feet. "Do you hear me?"

She smiled mistily and nodded.

While Jennifer was still absorbing the effects of Dave's massive tenderness, he turned to her. There was nothing gentle about the way he was reaching for her, she thought, stumbling back in surprise until her shoulders touched the dirt wall. Nothing indulgent or benign about his embrace. He swept her up in rock-hard arms and held her locked against him.

At first, all she could feel was his strength, his arms restraining her instinctive attempt at flight. Then, slowly, when her own clamoring reactions stilled and she let him take her weight, she felt his heat. Warmth seeped through her wet clothes, soaked deep into her bones, and she melted against him, wanting more. His pounding heart matched hers, beat for frantic beat. But the impact of his strength and warmth faded when she felt the tremors shuddering through his big body into hers.

"Oh, Dave," she whispered, "I'm so sorry."

He held her for a second more, then let her go. His dark eyes met hers for a charged moment. "Later," he said briefly. It was a promise. It was also a threat.

The cave wasn't any larger close up than it had looked from the trail, he decided after another quick glance around. In an emergency, three adults and a llama could be crammed in it together, but this wasn't exactly an emergency. His rig was less than a quarter of a mile away and could, in a pinch, bed down three. But he didn't like the idea of taking Tillie back out on the trail and he wasn't going to leave either woman here alone.

"David," Tillie said firmly, "you should do something right away about Jennifer. She's wet and cold."

He threw a harassed glance at her. "I *know* that," he bit out.

"I have a plan that will solve all of your problems," she told him, sending a speaking glance in Jennifer's direction. Resting her hand on the backpack he had propped against the wall, she said, "Leave me the foam pad that you have rolled up in here, and the sleeping bag. With that and something to nibble on, I'll be just fine until morning. There's enough wood to last the night and there's ample room for... Paladin and me."

The llama flattened his ears against his head and hummed dolefully.

"No." Dave's terse response was automatic. "I can't leave you out here alone."

"David," she said firmly, "one of the few perks of having ESP is knowing when I am safe. I can tell you without reservation that there is nothing on this mountain that will harm me."

Jennifer asked, "Are you sure, Aunt Tillie?"

The two women exchanged a long glance.

"Absolutely."

They turned to him, and Dave did what any other male would do when confronted with such a feminine alliance—he swore and began digging in the pack. Unrolling a foam pad, he spread it near the fire and covered it with a down sleeping bag.

"Are your clothes dry?" he demanded shortly.

"Oh, yes. Only my shoes were wet and Jennifer gave me dry socks. She's taken wonderful care of me."

"Too bad she didn't do the same for herself," he said in a biting voice.

Jennifer raised her eyes to the ceiling and reminded herself that his patience had been sorely tried for some hours.

After dropping a few food bars on the sleeping bag, Dave dug in the pack for one last item. He placed a whistle on a chain around Tillie's neck. "If you need me for anything," he said with a worried frown, "just blow on that and I'll be right here."

Patting his hand, she said, "You get a good rest, and I'll see you in the morning." With a shooing motion of her hands, she looked at the two of them and said, "Go!"

Dave slung the pack over one shoulder and clamped a hand around Jennifer's elbow. Once outside, beyond the light of the fire, he stopped, reminding himself that his name wasn't Richard. Fighting the impulse to pick her up and haul her back to the truck, he said, "You're a lady who likes to be consulted, so here are the choices I see. We can make a lean-to out here—hell, *you* can make it if you really want to—and we can bunk there for the night, or we can go back to the truck."

Jennifer looked at him in disbelief that verged on outrage. Wasn't that just like a man? She was wet, cold, dirty, hungry and tired and he was asking if she wanted to play pioneer woman and build a lean-to, whatever that was. She wasn't stupid enough to ask. As far as that went, she didn't care. For the first time in a long time, she was yearning to be coddled, to be spoiled rotten, and that feeling had to occur at the exact moment that he decided to be an enlightened male! Life was unfair, she decided dejectedly. And cruel.

"Look," she said firmly, squinting up at him through the fine mist, "if being in a lean-to means spending one more minute being wet and cold, forget it. I want to be warm. And dry. If you can get me that way, then do it! However you can. The sooner the better."

"Okay, honey, let's go. The truck isn't far." The smile in his voice made her wonder if she had been too hasty.

But nothing could have been more circumspect than Dave's solution. When they reached the truck, he stuffed her in the passenger door and went around to his side to start the motor. As warm air began gushing through the heater, he pulled her dry clothes out of the pack and said, "Drop your wet things on the floor and put these on. Call me when you're done." With that, he got out and slammed the door.

"Heat," she groaned, taking a moment to savor it. "Glorious heat!" Then she started working her way out of her snug jacket. While she struggled to peel off the wet clothes, Jennifer felt the truck bed shift and absently wondered what he was doing back there. The next instant she decided that she didn't care. Warmth filled the cab of the truck, and she reflected that Dave was a jewel among men—he had an eye for details. He had dropped some packages of moistened towelettes on top of her clothes, and after using them, she luxuriated in the sensation of being clean, as well as warm and dry.

There were advantages to Dave's size, she decided, pulling on a pair of cotton socks. The cab was roomy enough to make a decent dressing room. Once she was in a clean pair of jeans and a knit shirt, she reached the conclusion that it would also be ample for sleeping. A bit crowded with the two of them, but adequate.

Rolling down the window, she called, "Okay, you can come back now."

Dave opened her door. "Perfect timing," he said, swinging her up in his arms.

Jennifer gasped when the cool air hit her. "Dave," she wailed softly, clutching at his shoulders, "what are you doing? I just got warm."

His arms tightened. "Are you the same lady who turned things over to me a few minutes ago?" he asked, a waiting quality behind his slight grin.

"Yes," she answered doubtfully, not understanding the dark expression in his eyes.

"Do you trust me?"

There was no teasing smile this time. He wanted a straight answer.

"Yes," she said to remove his uncertainty. Then, to bring back the grin, she added, "But I'm not into masochism, so move!"

With a satisfied chuckle, he brought her closer to his chest and headed to the back of the truck. "Lift the flap," he directed, nodding at the tarp, "and climb in." She followed the first part of his instructions, then peeked in. A huge flashlight illuminated the interior and there on the bed of the truck was a huge, double-sized, down sleeping bag, waiting.

"Still trust me?" The words were spoken casually, but tension tightened his arms.

She didn't hesitate. "Yes." After crawling in, she sat and wiggled between the covers. Dave still waited, holding back the flap, simply watching. "Well," she said, a smile turning up the corners of her mouth, "are you coming in or not?"

Before Dave slid in the sleeping bag beside her, he stripped down to his briefs. Somewhere along the way, as he undressed, Jennifer turned off the flashlight. It was one thing, she acknowledged silently, to hear the rustling of his clothes in the dark. It was another thing entirely to watch him shed one item of clothing after another, to have a nearly nude, primitive-looking man emerge, a man who throughout the entire process, never took his eyes from hers!

"You're dressed modestly enough for both of us," he told her matter-of-factly as he pulled up the zipper of the sleeping bag. "Besides, my clothes were damp." Then he hauled her into his arms and held her, not saying a word. "Never," he ordered finally in a thick voice, "never, ever, do anything that crazy again. I lost about ten years of the new life that Doc Carter gave me."

"Tillie told me." She wrapped her arms around his neck and gave him a hug. "That's wonderful."

"She's got a big mouth," he grumbled. "I wanted to tell you myself."

They stayed that way for long, silent moments. Touching, cherishing, accepting. Finally, he said, "Why did you do it? Why didn't you wait for me?"

With a sigh, Jennifer rolled onto her back, tucking her head into the hollow of his shoulder. "Believe me," she said spiritedly, "I didn't want to go chasing after rustlers. But Aunt Tillie was determined, and I couldn't let her go alone."

Rearing up on one elbow, Dave stared down at her. "*Rustlers?* How in the hell—what do you *mean*, rustlers?"

"Shh." She patted his arm consolingly. "Tillie said they weren't very good ones, so you didn't miss much. In fact, she told me that they've already had an in-depth conversation with Nick and some of the others. Now, if you'll just settle down, I'll tell you all about it."

"But how did she know that something was going on?"

"The llamas, of course. Maybelle told her all about it."

Dave's only comment was one, pithy, Anglo-Saxon word. Jennifer gurgled with amusement, and he was so entranced with the muted sound of laughter in the dark, the shaking of her body against his, that he held back his questions. Only occasionally did he interrupt her outrageous story, when he couldn't contain himself any longer.

"But why was she determined to go after Paladin?"

Her voice was husky, quivering with amusement. "Are you ready for this?"

He groaned.

"Because Paladin has Walter's eyes and she thinks that he's—"

"Come *back*? No. Damn it, I don't believe it. You're making it up, aren't you?"

"Not a word of it," she assured him. "Anyway, she needed the time with him tonight so she could talk to him."

"She didn't have to come all the way up here to do that. She can talk to him every hour on the hour at the ranch."

"Not so." Jennifer solemnly explained about the "shield" Paladin had put up and Tillie's theory about his karma, and his harem. "And she's going to spend the night trying to get through to him, to worm the whole story out of him," she finished with a flourish.

"Wait a minute. Stop. Hold everything." Dave rolled onto his side and turned her to face him. "I'm beginning to get a little worried, here. You sound like you really believe this."

"Well," Jennifer drew out the word thoughtfully. "When I'm with her, she makes it sound so... ordinary."

"Yeah." His grin was a flash of white in the darkness. "Scary, isn't it?" After a thoughtful silence, he said, "Do you suppose ESP is a genetic thing? Do you think any of our children will have it?" His heart was thundering so loud that he was sure she would hear it.

"Are we going to have children?" she asked cautiously, her voice faint.

How could she not feel the pounding of his heart? he wondered. His next thought was that she hadn't kicked him out of the truck and out of her life. He had to take encouragement where he found it. "I'd like to," he said simply. "But before we get to that stage, you've got to understand and believe a few things about me."

She blinked. "Like what?"

"For starters, that I'm not Richard, and I never will be. That I want you to be happy and fulfilled. If teaching is what it takes, then I want you to teach. I don't like doormats, and we might fight like hell at times, but I'll love you all the more for standing up for what you believe."

"You love me?" Her voice quavered on the second word.

Never had he loved so fiercely as that moment. "Yep," he said casually, knowing instinctively that she had to find her way to him before he showed her just how much. "From the first time I saw you."

"What if I don't love you?" she whispered.

He shook his head slowly, brushing her lips with his each time he moved his head. His breath touched her cheek, her chin, her mouth. "There's no way on God's green earth that you couldn't love me," he whispered, moving his hand to her nape and bringing her face to his throat.

Jennifer's lips felt his pulse, then felt his life force invade her body, touch her bones, her very soul. Felt his words reach out and surround her, hold her close.

"You love me," he told her gently, "because somewhere, sometime we were made for each other. We're two halves of a whole. We belong together, and in time, we'll be a perfect fit."

They lay silently, her lips still touching his throat. Slowly, slowly, her body relaxed until she let him take her weight, support her.

Much later, tucked in the curve of his body like a spoon, she whispered, "Dave?"

"Mmm?"

"Are you awake?"

"No. What do you want?"

"I'm sorry, but you throw off heat like a furnace. I'm getting too warm."

He sighed and touched his lips to her ear. "You are a woman to try a man's soul. Come on, I'll help you get your pants off. Then maybe you'll go to sleep."

Smiling, she murmured, "Yes, David."

The next morning Dave drove down below the cave and went up to meet Tillie. Paladin had started down earlier, she explained as she hopped into the truck. The road was already drying and the day was summer warm.

Once, looking at the blue, cloudless sky, Jennifer commented idly, "The weather here is as unpredictable as it is in California."

"A bit colder in the winter," Dave said dryly, then shot her a worried frown.

"David," Tillie said, "now that we know you're just fine, I should be going home. I still don't understand what Walter was talking about, but it will all be clear someday, I'm sure."

"Umm," he agreed absently, thinking that the only problem he'd had with his heart was that he'd lost it and was waiting for it to be picked up and claimed.

Tillie turned to face him, her eyes brightening. "That must be it!" she exclaimed. "Walter must have known that you'd—"

He shook his head, then tilted it toward Jennifer who was looking out the window with an abstracted expression. Tillie followed his gaze, looked back at him and nodded.

"I must say," she began indignantly, "that he's going to have to sharpen his communication skills. To have me coming all the way out here and you spending all that time in the doctor's office is just too much. And," she finished darkly, "he'll probably try to blame the whole misunderstanding on me!"

Jennifer turned in time to catch the amused expression on Dave's face. "Am I missing something?"

Tillie smiled serenely. "We were just saying that Walter is going to have to clarify some of his statements in the future."

"Speaking of Walter," Jennifer said tentatively, "did you have a nice conversation last night? Or did you have any conversation at all?"

Tillie's blue eyes held a frustrated gleam. "Oh, we spoke, there was no problem about that. I talked to a llama all night," she said grimly. "A llama named Paladin. He told me what a responsibility it was to be a sire of a herd. Work, work, work, was his complaint. According to him, life was just one onerous duty after another."

"Hmm. If he had nothing to hide, why didn't he talk to you before?" Jennifer asked reasonably.

"He *said* that there are so many females in his life, he makes a point of isolating himself when he can. That he doesn't take part in idle chitchat." Her sniff said quite clearly what she thought of that.

"Makes sense to me," Dave said, smiling broadly when the two women glared at him. "The water's down," he said abruptly as they neared the bridge.

"I think I'll go see Maybelle, then call the airlines," Tillie murmured when they pulled up in front of Dave's place.

"I've got some things to do at the cabin," Jennifer told them both vaguely, staring through the windshield. He hadn't said a word to her this morning, she reflected miserably. How much of what he'd said the night before could be chalked up to anxiety and stress? And even if he'd meant every word of it, what did *she* want? This was the summer of her brave new beginning—the time to get her credential renewed, go back to teaching, savor the life of a young, single professional. Single being the operative word. Single, meaning free, unattached, responsible to no one but herself.

She jumped when Dave came around to her side. He was standing too close, she fretted, sliding down and finding herself pinned between him and the door. He kept her there while he extended a hand to Tillie, helping her down and waiting until Tillie patted his arm and moved away. Then he turned and laced his fingers through Jennifer's hair, his palms framing her face.

His lips covered hers in a possessive kiss that she felt all the way down to her toes. When her eyes opened and met his, she knew. It hadn't been stress. He'd meant every word he'd said. So that put the ball in her court.

His mouth touched hers again, lingered, then reluctantly lifted. "I'm going to see Nick to make sure that everyone's okay, then I'll wait for you at my place."

Her eyes widened anxiously. "But, I might not . . . I don't know . . . For how long?"

"As long as it takes." He brushed her bottom lip with his thumb, just a shadow of a touch, then left.

Once inside her cabin, Jennifer headed straight for the bathroom and took a long, hot shower and washed her hair. That used up about fifteen minutes. Drying her hair and dressing took another ten. She ate an orange, pretended to work, roamed around the cabin and looked out the window at Dave's house. She watched the sun move across the sky and the shadows lengthen. By dinnertime, the sun was setting and she was hungry and verging on panic. She pictured Dave, waiting as he'd promised, while she wrestled with questions.

Did she still want to teach?

Yes.

Just how important was it?

She didn't know.

Could she live outside of California?

Probably.

Could she tolerate Montana winters?

They sounded scary.

Did she want to get married again?

That was even scarier.

Did she love Dave?

What was love? She thought she had known when she'd married Richard. She was back to scary.

Did she trust Dave?

With her life. That was the one thing—the only thing—of which she was completely certain. There was a vast difference between the two men, she realized, putting her thoughts into words for the first time. While Richard had given what *he*'d thought was good for her, Dave's offerings were merely to fulfill her needs and wants.

A massive difference. And, she realized suddenly, a better starting place than most people had. Before she could change her mind, she walked out the door and started across the grassy incline. Halfway there, she broke into a run.

"Dave!" She rapped on the screen door. There was no light inside. What if he hadn't waited? "Dave?"

"In here." His calm voice brushed away her sudden fear. When she stepped inside, she saw him sitting on the couch by the windows and knew that he must have witnessed her mad sprint across the grass. He opened his arms in mute invitation. "You probably saved my sanity," he groaned as she sat down in his lap. Wrapping his arms around her, he gave her a convulsive hug. "The later it got, the more scared I got."

"I was frightened," she told him, rubbing her cheek on his shoulder.

"I know."

"I made such a mess of things the first time, I—"

He put his finger across her lips, stopping her. "What's my name?"

She gave him a wry smile. "Dave. David."

"My full name."

"David McGraw."

"Good." He nodded in satisfaction. "You'll be sure and remember?"

"I won't forget," she promised, her smile spreading. "How bad are your winters here?" she asked abruptly.

His heart jumped and he held her tighter. "Bad," he admitted. "But I won't make you go out in the snow and milk the cows. I'll keep you as warm as you want to be."

"About my teaching—"

"The only problem I see is that we might get snowed in at times."

"You wouldn't change your mind later?"

"What'd we agree my name was?"

Jennifer smiled, her arms sliding around his neck. "Aunt Tillie said that David means 'beloved,'" she informed him languidly.

His brows rose. "Am I your beloved?"

She hesitated. "Could I answer that later?"

He nodded, pressing deeper into the couch, taking her with him, knowing that when he'd wrung that answer out of her, he'd have everything he wanted. "I've been thinking."

"Oh?"

"About you being such a stubborn woman and all."

She smiled, touching her lips to his neck, waiting to feel his body jolt. When she did, her smile grew broader. "I love it when you go all cowboy on me," she confided.

"Stubborn," he repeated tenaciously. "About things like accepting help."

She stiffened.

"So I decided that I'll just tell the men that helping you is forbidden. If they want to hustle for a raise, they can try things like letting the air out of your tires and watching you pump them back up. With a hand pump, of course." He felt her go boneless against him, her warm breath on his neck.

"Of course."

"Or put roadblocks up to keep your students away."

"I could try substitute teaching," she mused. "That way, I wouldn't have to worry about being snowed in."

"See what a perverse woman you are?" he pointed out, his heart pounding so fast he could hardly breathe. "The meaner I get, the more you try to move in on me. We'll make you fix your own dinner."

"We could keep the literacy center here."

"Then there's always the haying."

"An extra phone in the house would be helpful, but I could live without it."

"We always need another strong back when we're out in the fields."

"It would make it easier when the children come."

He blinked. "We're having children?"

She flexed like a cat against his big body, feeling his love pour over her. "After the honeymoon," she promised.

He touched her lips with his. "When's that?"

The tip of her tongue brushed his. "After the wedding."

"When's that?" He bent his head again.

She sighed. "After the proposal."

He shook his head. "I've got my work cut out for me."

"You do indeed."

"Will you?" he asked, taking a deep breath.

"Will I what?" Her eyes laughed at him.

"Marry me?"

Serious now, she said, "Yes. Oh, yes."

The kiss that followed was long and hot, desperate and relieved.

"Definitely," she murmured, when she could get her breath.

"What?"

"David," she whispered. "My beloved."

*   *   *   *   *

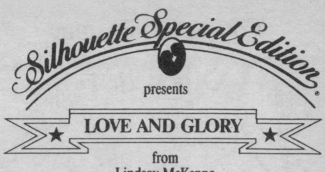

Silhouette Special Edition

presents

★ LOVE AND GLORY ★

from
Lindsay McKenna

Introducing a gripping new series celebrating our men—and women—in uniform. Meet the Trayherns, a military family as proud and colorful as the American flag, a family fighting the shadow of dishonor, a family determined to triumph—with
LOVE AND GLORY!

June: **A QUESTION OF HONOR** (SE #529) leads the fast-paced excitement. When Coast Guard officer Noah Trayhern offers Kit Anderson a safe house, he unwittingly endangers his own guarded emotions.

July: **NO SURRENDER** (SE #535) Navy pilot Alyssa Trayhern's assignment with arrogant jet jockey Clay Cantrell threatens her career—and her heart—with a crash landing!

August: **RETURN OF A HERO** (SE #541) Strike up the band to welcome home a man whose top-secret reappearance will make headline news . . . with a delicate, daring woman by his side.

Silhouette Intimate Moments

NOW APPEARING!

LIEUTENANT GABRIEL RODRIGUEZ
in
Something of Heaven

From his first appearance in Marilyn Pappano's popular *Guilt by Association*, Lieutenant Gabriel Rodriguez captured readers' hearts. Your letters poured in, asking to see this dynamic man reappear—this time as the hero of his own book. This month, all your wishes come true in *Something of Heaven* (IM #294), Marilyn Pappano's latest romantic tour de force.

Gabriel longs to win back the love of Rachel Martinez, who once filled his arms and brought beauty to his lonely nights. Then he drove her away, unable to face the power of his feelings and the cruelty of fate. That same fate has given him a second chance with Rachel, but to take advantage of it, he will have to trust her with his darkest secret: somewhere in the world, Gabriel may have a son. Long before he knew Rachel, there was another woman, a woman who repaid his love with lies—and ran away to bear their child alone. Rachel is the only one who can find that child for him, but if he asks her, will he lose her love forever or, together, will they find *Something of Heaven*?

This month only, read *Something of Heaven* and follow Gabriel on the road to happiness.

Silhouette Intimate Moments
Where the Romance Never Ends

IM294-1A

Silhouette Intimate Moments®

NORA ROBERTS
brings you the first
Award of Excellence title
Gabriel's Angel
coming in August from
Silhouette Intimate Moments

They were on a collision course with love....

Laura Malone was alone, scared—and pregnant. She was running for the sake of her child. Gabriel Bradley had his own problems. He had neither the need nor the inclination to get involved in someone else's.

But Laura was like no other woman ... and she needed him. Soon Gabe was willing to risk all for the heaven of her arms.

The Award of Excellence is given to one specially selected title per month. Look for the second Award of Excellence title, coming out in September from Silhouette Romance—**SUTTON'S WAY** by **Diana Palmer**

Im 300-1

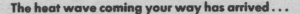